The sensation in the zero-gravity tank was dream-like. Everything was very slow, as if the tank were filled with half-firm Jell-O. Nathan was drifting, comfortable in a way he had never been before. And the space! Without any feeling at all that one way was "up" and another "down," every side of the tank was useful. Suddenly he understood that in a spaceship the ceiling really was the same as the floor or the walls, and that gave it four times as much usable space.

And furniture wasn't necessary. Sitting was no more comfortable than floating in any other position.

"Try to reach the shuttle mock-up," a voice came through in his helmet.

But every time Nathan moved an arm or leg, his whole body swung slowly in the opposite direction. Pretty soon he was all twisted up and getting nowhere.

All right. There had to be a way to do this. Nathan positioned himself so that he was headed toward the mock door like an arrow. He raised his arms very very slowly, trying to negate as much of the back-push as he could. Then he swooped down with some force, which propelled him forward.

"Very good," said the voice.

Nathan felt he was one step closer to going to Mars. . . .

JACK ANDERSON PRESENTS...

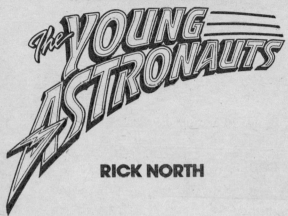

RICK NORTH

ZEBRA BOOKS
KENSINGTON PUBLISHING CORP.

RL 5.6, IL age 10 and up

ZEBRA BOOKS

are published by

Kensington Publishing Corp.
475 Park Avenue South
New York, NY 10016

First printing: July, 1990

Printed in the United States of America

To Christa McAuliffe, who reached out to the stars.

Dear Reader:

Aboard the Soviet Space Station MIR, I have had the opportunity to reflect on the incomparable beauty of our planet Earth. From space one cannot see national boundaries that define the countries of our planet. One can only realize how precious the Earth is to all people.

To live in space is to realize the common interest of humankind and the opportunities of exploration that will present themselves in the next century to all of our children.

In the spirit of MIR, which is the Russian word for peace, I encourage every student of science to prepare for their opportunity to travel in space. Each of us should work to expand our knowledge of the universe and to enrich our lives on our planet.

Peace through space to children everywhere!

Alexander Serebrov
Cosmonaut-Hero of the
Soviet Union

Written in orbit
aboard Soviet Space Station MIR.
April 1990

Part I:
May

Chapter One

USA: Nathan

A skinny envelope meant bad news. Nathan could tell just from the feel that there wasn't more than one sheet inside. That, and the return address. Not Houston or Star City, but Geneva. Whoever heard of a space program run out of Geneva? Maybe it was something else, another request for copies of his test scores, his medical evaluations, or the endless sessions with the shrink.

"Move it, Long. I'm getting old waiting," Eddie called from the front step.

"I'm coming," Nathan yelled back through the screen door. He didn't move. The letter lay in his hand. He recognized the crest of the UN's Mars program from each of the earlier rounds. He swallowed hard. His acceptance to the program meant so much to Nathan and his mother, and if the news was disappointing, all the dreams they had been building together would be destroyed.

The Mars program was a miracle, Nathan thought.

Just last year, when his mother finally sat down with the school counselor and began to talk about the money part of college, things had looked bad.

"For a student like Nathan," the counselor had said, "getting into a top school will be no problem. As a matter of fact, CalTech, Stanford, and Princeton have already asked about him. And they don't ask without promising full scholarships."

A little smile had settled on his mom's face, and that had made him happy. Proud that he could put that smile there when no one else could.

"But that won't cover books and room and board," the counselor had continued. "And, unfortunately, Ms. Long, your earnings are just over the cutoff for government loan assistance."

His mother's eyes had snapped at that. "We'll just see," was all she said. Later that night Nathan had heard her crying in her bedroom. He had thought of going in, maybe telling her that they could work it out, they always had worked it out before. But there wasn't anything he could say that night. Maybe his father would help, but he knew that his mother didn't want to ask. Since the divorce he'd seen his father twice. He didn't really think asking the man for money was the answer. Dad had never come through for them before. And then the Mars program came out of nowhere like a miracle.

"All you have to do is make the final cut," the interviewer said. "Even if you don't make the group selected for Mars, your entire education will still be picked up by the UN as long as you are willing to work on the Earth-mission program for five years after graduation. It's a good deal."

10

It was a great deal, an awesome deal. The Earth-mission program was plenty hot with lots of room for advanced work. And they were offering good salaries. Only it was based in Australia, and no matter how ready he was to leave home, he didn't think he'd want to leave his mom alone that far away.

A little skate-rat attitude crept in, borrowed from Eddie and the other thrashers he hung around with. "My mom's a bookkeeper. Could you give her a job too?"

The interviewer laughed heartily and said he liked Nathan's attitude. Nathan found that a little hard to take. Most adults seemed upset that he could be so smart and so . . . so *adolescent* at the same time. Teachers seemed to forget that even though he could whip strings around them in calculus and chemistry, he was still a teenager. And he was not about to fall for the dweeb stereotype of a brain. No way. Not when he could do some pretty radical airs on his skateboard.

Well, maybe he wasn't ready to pierce an ear like Eddie, although he thought it looked kind of cool. But his hair was long enough that his math teacher kept after him all the time. Until he got fed up and used about half a pound of Eddie's mousse to create the effect that he had stuck his finger in an electrical socket. When Mr. Jordan complained, Nathan had meekly asked whether he shouldn't try to emulate Einstein. That had gotten him sent to the office.

"I'm gonna be ready for retirement by the time you get out here," Eddie yelled again.

Nathan swallowed hard. If he waited much longer, then Eddie would be gone, and he didn't want to be alone no matter what the news was. His mom's boss was a real pig about personal phone calls. Gently he slid a finger under the flap and pulled the thing open.

We are pleased to inform you that Mr. Nathan Long has been accepted to the Mars preflight program in Houston, Texas. He should be prepared to report September 17. More information will follow under separate cover.

There was more, but Nathan couldn't read it. He could barely make out the words in front of him. Adrenaline seemed to seep even into his eyeballs. The impact was loud and explosive.

"Aw *riiight!!!!*"

"What happened?" Eddie burst in and left the screen door flapping. "I miss something? You win the lottery, Nate-head?"

"Yeah," Nathan said. "The lottery. Yeah."

"Well, if that means you're too rich to bother working on that jump, I'll be going. I got things to do."

"Wait," Nathan said, catching Eddie's sleeve. "I'm getting my 'board now, okay? I want to get that jump turn down."

Before I go, he added to himself. But there was a whole summer before September 17. Until twenty minutes ago it seemed like the summer was going to be too short. Now it stretched out into forever.

USSR: Sergei

Sergei Mikhailovich Chuvakin hesitated before knocking on the polished wooden door to the office. Everyone in the class had stared at him when he had been summoned in the middle of Russian lit, which he had taken to be a good sign. He hated Russian lit. It

12

wasn't like chemistry or physics or geometry, where things were right or wrong and the answers were clear and pure and logical. No, people in stories were always decidedly illogical, and no matter how many times Miss Palshina talked about motivation and options, Sergei still couldn't believe that any of it made sense. Yes, that was a good sign.

But he still hesitated, because how good could it be? He already knew that he hadn't made it. His grades in the relevant subjects were high enough, and his medical records and psychiatric evaluations were all excellent, but there was the small matter of a few less than perfect grades in literature and the time he had been caught pinning a really stupid sign to Svetlana's red Young Pioneers scarf. But that had been all the way back in sixth grade, and she had been the prettiest girl in the class. She had refused to talk to him ever again, which had hurt badly. Sergei counted his blessings. At least she didn't attend the Leningrad Academy of Science, or else none of the girls here would talk to him either.

Which all led to the fact that four pictures went up in the main lobby across from the portrait of Lenin before first period this morning and none of them had been his. There had been a beautifully lettered sign too, *Leningrad Science Academy students selected for the Mars program*, and under that the slogan "To Mars Together" written in all five official languages of the UN. Ludmilla, of course, and Alexei Ivanovich and Alla Romashko. But to see Grigori Kurashov smiling down from that position of honor, that made his face hot and his stomach clench. He was better than Kurashov, always had been since they had been in kindergarten together. Sure,

13

Kurashov had beaten him when they had been on opposing hockey teams, but Sergei didn't take all the blame for that. Two of their best players had been out, one with an injury and one with the flu.

And it wasn't even his fault. Grigori had always resented Sergei's ease in the hard classes, even before he resented his way with girls. The fact that Sergei, with his blond hair and high cheekbones, looked like a teen idol while Grigori was more hulking than athletic didn't help either. Even the fact that Kurashov could beat him in almost any sport didn't make up the difference.

The anger at Grigori had helped him through the first fifteen minutes of the day, until the cold realization hit in full force. His picture wasn't up there. He wasn't going. And even though he was sixteen years old and not a kid anymore, hot tears flooded his eyes. He didn't let them fall. Instead, he looked down and studied the map on his desk through his tears.

All his life he had wanted only one thing—to be a cosmonaut. It was a silly dream, everyone had said. Every little kid dreams of it the same way they dream of being great ballet stars and heroes in the Great Patriotic War. Later, they promised, he would grow out of it and dream of other things, of being a scientist or professor or engineer. Something reasonable and practical and useful. "They" all seemed to forget that some people did actually grow up to be cosmonauts and ballet stars. The kids who didn't let go of the dream.

So he had remained very quiet about his dream and let the grown-ups think it had died. He had kept it glowing, alive and secret, careful where his pursuit would take him. For the dream alone he had studied hard, harder than his schoolmates, had joined the As-

14

tronomy Club and the Chemistry Club and the Young Cosmonauts and the hockey league at the Pioneer Palace. He had done all the right things — except he had to go and tease the girls and could not understand why people in novels insisted on doing stupid things like whining for three hundred pages instead of just getting a divorce. Stuff like that.

Now it was all over and they were going to tell him that. He felt alone and scared, more scared than he had ever been in his life. So he knocked on the solid wood with a feeling of doom.

The door opened and he was led past the secretaries, past the student barrier, and into the inner office. He didn't see any of it. His eyes were glued firmly to the washed-out gray tile floor waxed so brightly he could see his own face in it. He wiped his palms on his uniform pants before he looked up. Dr. Yagudin smiled broadly. There were two other men in the room with him, and they weren't smiling at all.

"First of all, Sergei Mikhailovich, I wish to congratulate you. We have been informed that you have been chosen for the final Mars-project group. Naturally we could not be more pleased."

"But . . ." Sergei stuttered, his eyes flashing. "What about this morning . . . ?" He was so puzzled that he felt dizzy.

"We are afraid there might have been a little confusion," one of the other men said. "You have been accepted to the final phase of the selection process, but the committee has indicated that you will be going to the Houston center instead of to our own Star City. We had wanted to rectify any mistake before making a public announcement."

15

Sergei wanted to laugh, to jump on the upholstered armchairs, to do cartwheels down the hall. To be so miserable one moment and reprieved the next was a shock to his system. At least one full-bodied whoop came out before he managed to get back under control. After all, he was sixteen and a young adult. Not a little kid anymore.

So he waited until he felt just a little more in control before he spoke. "If I don't go, someone else will have to," he said reasonably enough. "That wouldn't be fair."

The strange men both nodded and Dr. Yagudin smiled with pride. "That's very mature of you, Sergei," the principal said. "But I suppose you wouldn't have been chosen unless you had demonstrated qualities besides your intellectual gifts."

Sergei had the grace to blush. It wasn't simply the compliment. He was used to that. No, it was because he was being praised for the wrong thing. The men and Dr. Yagudin didn't know about Ludmilla and Raisa, who were the real reasons that Sergei had hoped so desperately to be sent to Houston. Or anywhere but Star City.

He had met Raisa at camp two years earlier, both of them in the young cosmonaut program. She was very pretty, with heavy dark hair and large eyes, just the opposite of Ludmilla. And she was the best student of the group, too, his very worst competition. They had started out like a pair of duelists, always trying to score off each other, until the night he had led the boys' raid on the kitchen. He'd found Raisa there already with half the girls' bunk.

They'd met at camp again the previous year and they wrote often. Sergei knew that Raisa thought that she

16

was his girlfriend, and had said enough about that in her last two letters. How they would have so much fun together in Star City. He had never told her about Ludmilla. And if Raisa and Ludmilla were both in Star City, then Sergei knew that he was in hot water.

One of the unfamiliar men had been saying something Sergei didn't quite follow, something about when to report and regulations and informing his parents and the rest. "Forget it," the second man said. "This isn't the time. Let him get used to the news first."

The second man shrugged and they left. Then the bell rang. "You may go, Sergei," Dr. Yagudin said kindly.

Sergei slipped out of the office. Where there had been four pictures across from the portrait of Lenin there were now five. The office had been fast, that was sure. As Sergei stood, mesmerized and not quite sure what to believe of it all, Ludmilla came up behind him and tapped him on the shoulder.

"I was so worried this morning," she said rapidly. "I knew there had to be some mistake, that you had to be going too. I knew it. And everyone said we were such babies to really be hoping. . . . And now it's true, Sergei. And we're both going."

She slipped her books into his hands and buttoned up her coat. Her long blond braids swung over her shoulders, and Sergei could smell the clean shampoo. He hefted the books and they left the building through the main door, out through the gates, and down the street to the bus stop.

"It's not all finished yet," Sergei said carefully. "This is just the last cut, that's all. Not everyone is going."

Ludmilla blinked. "No. But *we* are."

17

The determination in her voice echoed the feeling that overwhelmed him. *He* was going. There was no mistake about that. None at all.

Sergei smiled slowly. "*We're* going," he said again. "But they can keep Grigori."

Ludmilla laughed with him as they walked to the bus stop. He wanted to take her hand, but that wasn't a good idea this close to school. Some of the younger kids might see them. And besides, she was wearing gloves.

The bus pulled up. "I'll see you tomorrow," he yelled as she got on. And then she was gone. That was fine. Now Ludmilla and Raisa would never find out about each other, and that was just how Sergei wanted it to be.

He walked down the street toward the river. It was May and warm enough to walk, and he wanted to be alone. Too much had happened in one day. Mars. Houston. Rejection and acceptance all at the same time. Sergei Mikhailovich stared down into the thick gray water and tried to make it reality. Going to the United States. Going to Mars.

Somehow he wasn't sure that he wouldn't just wake up.

Venezuela: Noemi

Early May hid the first touches of autumn in Caracas, but Noemi Tejas y Velazquez thought she could smell the first touches of the coming winter in the air. Nothing really noticeable, but the idea was there. Summer was gone.

She stepped out of her Sacred Heart School uniform and left it in the middle of the carpet. Her mother said that she shouldn't do that to the maid, that the house-

18

keeper had enough of a job without picking up after a young lady who was very soon going to be old enough to run a house of her own. Noemi didn't care.

She put on a pair of jeans and a white blouse and flopped on the bed. Her pink Princess phone stood out invitingly on the expanse of pale rose carpet. She wanted to call Soledad and Suzanne and tell them how horrible Miss Amaya had been again. But Suzanne and Soledad weren't back from Milan yet, and when they returned they would tell her all about the latest fashions and model them all and wouldn't care in the least that Noemi had been fighting everybody to get into the graduate algebra courses. They always laughed when she told them about it. *Why do you want to bother?* they always asked her. *If the boys think you're too smart, they won't be interested.*

Noemi had always worried about that in secret. Her mother, along with her friends, had worried aloud. And Flora, the housekeeper, had worried more than all the others combined. But at least her father was rich enough that someone would be interested in her money, and she was pretty enough. And being too smart wasn't a major disadvantage at Sacred Heart, where there were no boys to find out anyway.

The problem was, she was more than qualified to take the course in group theory. She liked algebra. It was very much like fashion, beautiful and utterly useless. And school was boring, boring, boring. She didn't know why she didn't just leave, spend her time with her books and computer and her friends and her credit cards. That made much more sense than sitting around falling asleep while Sister Ana Luz lectured about the steady-state theory. No one believed that anymore.

Even the most vigorous detractors now accepted that the universe began in the big bang. There were the radio signals to prove it, and even the church was completely in agreement.

Noemi stared at the ceiling and felt as if she were fighting an unjust and extremely biased universe. It wasn't fair. Just because she was fifteen she needed her parents' permission to take a math class. And she had their permission. They had called Mother Dolores, the principal of Sacred Heart. But Miss Amaya had been a brick wall. Not unless her father came down and signed the paper in front of her was she going to permit Noemi to register for any classes at the university. Finished. The end.

A soft knock on the door brought her attention back to the present. "I have something for you, Noemita. Something you want."

Flora. Not even her father called her Noemita, at least not anymore. Noemi couldn't tell whether the housekeeper was talking about a message or a cup of hot chocolate. Flora used the same tone she had used when Noemi was just learning to walk — and refused to believe that the baby had grown.

Noemi rolled off the bed and opened the door. Flora, beaming, proffered a silver tray with a single letter on it. Noemi made a little face. She wasn't expecting any letter, and it couldn't be anyone she wanted to hear from anyway. Neither Soledad nor Suzanne ever wrote, and the return address wasn't Milan.

It was Geneva.

Her eyes grew wide as she picked up the envelope. She hadn't been expecting it so soon. She tore it open nervously, trying to ignore Flora constantly asking,

20

"What did they say? What did they say?"

She closed her eyes briefly and read it again. And then jumped and hugged the ancient housekeeper hard. "I'm going," she yelled to Flora and the world. "I'm going."

"Your mama will be so happy," Flora said.

Noemi froze in the middle of her rose-colored carpet. She hadn't exactly told her parents. She had given them all the forms to sign, and they had signed away the same as they had always signed anything she had asked for. Like credit card statements and telephone bills and requests to transfer classes. She had never really thought about it before, and suddenly realized that she was going to have to explain something. And she was afraid.

She could just imagine telling her father. "It's a great honor, Daddy. Less than one percent were accepted, and this isn't even the final group. Only the last step in the process."

He would smile sadly and shake his head. "I would prefer other honors. Like your invitation to the charity ball. And an engagement. I would like that better."

Always, no matter what she did, he would prefer something more . . . more normal. And her mother would cock her head to one side and listen for a moment and then wonder what they were wearing in Houston these days and whether there was any decent shopping. And she would probably advise Noemi to stick to Italian designs no matter what they were wearing in Houston.

It made her furious and it made her sick and it made her want to shop.

Flora patted her shoulder, then spotted something

21

and left Noemi's side. The housekeeper picked up the discarded uniform and draped it over her arm. She looked back at Noemi, and her old face was deeply disappointed.

"You can go to Mars," the old woman said thoughtfully, "but you still can't pick up your clothes."

Chapter Two

Germany: Karl

Karl Muller was lost. His body was in his own room with a book open on his desk and a cheerful May breeze at the window. His mind was on the autobahn between Düsseldorf and Frankfurt. It had been Christmastime, and the snow had been wet and heavy on the trees, weighing down the boughs so that all the drive looked like an enchanted fairyland. They had spent every moment they could at his sister's new house with her new husband and her new grown-up life. Karl's older brother, Peter, had brought a foreign student with him from the university to celebrate the holidays. After all, no one should be alone at Christmas.

Karl thought it had been the best Christmas of his life. His life was perfect at that moment as they sped down the autobahn. He remembered quite clearly that he had been dozing against the door, watching his father's head as he drove, thinking about the whole Mars project. Dreaming of his acceptance, actually.

He had been afraid to tell Peter at first. His older

brother always seemed so much more capable than he was at everything. So he had waited, hesitated, until his father had insisted in front of all the relatives and his sisters in-law and even the foreign student, to tell everyone about it. He remembered being very proud and very self-conscious at the same time.

"We didn't even know about the first three eliminations," he told them shyly. "That was done by the schools and district panels. We weren't told much about that phase. Then maybe seven students in the district were asked if we wanted, to apply, which meant more tests and evaluations. Tests! I never thought there were so many tests. Subject matter, abstract reasoning, even personality screening. And we had to see a psychologist. And then there was the interview and then more tests again."

"Sounds like getting into college," the foreign student said.

"What about athletics?" his brother-in-law asked. That made sense. His brother-in-law managed a health club.

Karl had nodded. He'd been busy eating while the others talked, and his mouth was full of noodles and gravy.

"I didn't think I'd do so well on that," he admitted after he swallowed. "But they weren't looking for star athletes. More good health and good balance and general conditioning. They don't want to take the Olympic team."

"No, you'll give us a few more chances at medals before Mars enters their first Olympics," his brother-in-law joked. "But until then, please, feel free to come by the club and work out anytime. A little extra effort won't go to waste."

Karl had smiled at that. He hadn't known Ulrich well, but the visit had changed that. Now it was as if he had two older brothers instead of one. And while Ulrich ragged him almost as much as Peter, he also was generous and interested in Karl.

But most of all he remembered his mother, how she had smiled at them all and enjoyed that Christmas dinner. How, very softly, she had joked with Karl and Ulrich that night. "When it looks like a market for zero-G health clubs is about to break, I'm sure Karl will let you know. You can get a jump on the competition." Her voice had been low and soft, but they had all laughed. And he remembered later that night, the ambulance sirens and all the blood and how he had thought and prayed that it wasn't real at all.

He didn't remember much about the accident. Only that one moment they were driving along the dark, snowy highway. Karl vaguely remembered the lights in the windshield, powerful, breaking through the mist. After that were only snatches of sound, the ambulance and the police radio and what he later learned were metal shears opening the door. He remembered that, and the pain.

He hadn't really been hurt. Nothing a few stitches and tape and time couldn't put right. They kept him sedated anyway, for two days for "observation." It wasn't until he came out from under the painkilling drugs that his father told him. His mother was . . . gone. They had an agreement, his father and he did. In the five months that had passed, neither of them had ever used the word *dead*.

Karl had gone back to school, to the best semester he

25

had ever had. School was an escape from remembering. It was easier to take salami to his room and slice it off while he studied than to face the dining room table with one chair so glaringly empty. It was easier to study than to face his friends, their sympathy and their curiosity. It was easier to go right to the pool as soon as classes were over and swim laps until he could hardly breathe and his legs and chest burned. That way he didn't have to explain why he didn't walk home with his friends and spend lazy afternoons in Claus's darkroom or listening to Fritz's collection of rock tapes.

Karl felt the tears gathering in his eyes. Firmly he pulled his mind away from the memories, from the frightened emptiness inside, and forced himself to focus on the page. Heisenberg's "uncertainty principle." It is not possible to know both the velocity and position of an electron. The photon that reveals its position also increases its energy and thus changes the velocity. Karl read it through three times, trying to visualize the electron zipping through the dark, being zapped all around with particles of light. One finally hits, *zowie,* and there's the electron, all lit up. *Bam. Pow.* Just the way he used to draw war cartoons when he was a little kid.

He was so busy in the subatomic universe that he didn't hear the knock on his door. It came again, impatient, and this time it penetrated Karl's concentration. He jumped up and found his father waiting for him in the hall, an envelope in his hand. That was strange. His father shouldn't be home this early. Unless it was later than he thought, unless time had slipped away while he was lost in his own musings. That happened a lot since Christmas, that time dragged and sped up all at the same time and he was always surprised at how late or early it was.

"This came for you," his father said, holding out the envelope.

He saw the hope and the age in his father's face. He had gotten years older since the accident, his back stooping a bit and his eyes drooping and red. Karl swallowed hard and took the envelope. He knew what it was but he didn't, for a moment, know what to hope, or if he even cared. He tore the paper clumsily and read it over twice.

"Well?" his father asked.

Karl shrugged. "They accepted me for Houston. In September. If I go."

The words were out. Karl knew he didn't really care anymore, and was afraid to leave his father all alone. Afraid to leave his own place, his room, his school, the old friends who knew not to ask too much or impose on him in any way.

But his father stood smiling for the first time since Christmas. "That's wonderful, Karl. What do you mean, if you go? Of course you want to go."

"But . . ." Karl started to protest.

His father shook his head. "Your mother would have been so proud," the old man said softly. "Come, let's have a drink to celebrate."

As Karl Muller followed his father into the dining room, where the schnapps was kept, he felt the carefully hoarded tears start to fall.

New Zealand: Alice

"Alice is a Martian, Alice is a Martian," her five-year-old brother, Bobby, chanted. Alice Frances Thorne was ready to swat the little pest. He hadn't quit

27

even with their mother's threats, which never stopped Bobby anyhow. Now he grabbed the letter from her and ran, waving it like a flag.

"Give that back," Alice screamed, and then plunged after him. Knowing Bobby, he would dump it in the garbage or down the storm drain.

Bobby glanced behind and laughed. He ran out of the house, down the front road, and then across the field that was thick and slippery with new grass. Alice knew he was heading for the summer pasture, though they had gotten the sheep out nearly a month before.

"I'm gonna tell William," Bobby screeched.

Alice threw her hands up in disgust. Telling William was fine. She wouldn't have minded telling the foreman herself, as he could be trusted to handle Bobby and get the letter back as well. Bobby didn't listen to anyone the way he did to the ancient shepherd.

Instead, she stopped where she was, in the middle of the emerald grass field, and breathed in the scent of the late afternoon. In the distance she could see the flock like a woolly cloud settled on the ground. Behind them rose the mountains, purple-gray in the distance. A lump rose in her throat. No matter how much she told herself she wanted to be the best, do the best, she didn't honestly know how she was going to leave.

She heard the wheezing engine of her father's old truck as it turned into the lane to the house. He had been out buying barbed wire and new posts to fix the fence by the cliff and reinforce it before winter came. She didn't look down, didn't watch her father climb from the truck as it came to a full stop in front of the door, didn't watch her mother calmly offer a cup of hot coffee in a thick white mug.

28

She heard Joe and Lucy, the twins, slam the screened kitchen door. Probably Bobby had told them all, since the twins spent every afternoon in good weather with William and his two dogs. How often had her father said that Joe and Lucy had been born New Zealand sheep ranchers. And Bobby was picking up right after them. Alice had always felt like crying then, when he looked at her. She had never quite belonged like the others, belonged to the land and the sheep, to the shepherds and the people in the small town when they went to school and church and to buy supplies.

"She'll be off to university one day, that one will," the rector had said.

Her parents had agreed. And they had said it themselves more than once, trying to mix pride with the sadness they couldn't contain. "Off to university" was not exactly common here, where everyone was mostly concerned with the sheep and the weather and the price of wool and whether Mr. Sherman was finally going to marry Miss Ansazi.

Alice knew that she had to go on with her education, but she had also always assumed that she would come back home. A schoolteacher, perhaps, or a doctor or a veterinarian. And she would buy one of the white houses in town and have starched curtains like her mother and drive a weather-beaten old Ford pickup. And Sundays she would go home and have dinner with her parents and her brothers and sister and she would hear all the latest gossip from town. And now . . .

She looked out to the fading hills, to the brilliant rich color of the earth and sky around her. How could she ever leave?

She smelled the coffee first, before she felt the large,

gentle hand on her shoulder. Her father still patted her like the little ones, like the sheep and the funny, unstable lambs.

"You've done a fine thing," her father said. "And you belong out there in the world. Always did. But I don't know how we're going to do without you."

The lump that had been growing in Alice's throat rose. She turned and buried her face in her father's shoulder to hide the tears. Her father smoothed her long blond hair, hair just like her mother used to have before time and children turned it gray.

"Hey now, Alice, you're just like your grandmother Frances, who came over here as a young girl just after the war. All alone and afraid, she came to start a new life here in New Zealand. You're named for her, you know that. And you know the name Frances means 'free.' It's in your nature to go. It's in your destiny."

She nodded and wiped her eyes on her father's plaid flannel shirt, soft and faded from a hundred washings. Then she gave him a wan smile. After all, she knew she didn't have to decide just then. She might not even make the final crew. She was in the selection; that was all. Someday she would come back to these mountains, to the rich scent of the pastures, and to her family. Someday, somehow, she would return.

Chapter Three

Japan: Gen

The woman waiting patiently in the school office looked calm. She sat in a straight chair, her purse held on her lap in both hands. Her clothes were the latest Italian fashion and her black hair had been done in the latest Western style. She could be the mother of any student in Tokyo's Peer's School. But she was Genshiro Akamasu's mother, which meant that no matter how expensive her clothes and how calm she appeared, the secretary felt sorry for her.

They had buzzed the classroom twice. The secretary waited a little longer, putting off the unpleasant chore. Mrs. Akamasu stared at a spot on the wall.

"I'm very sorry, Mrs. Akamasu," the secretary finally said. "He isn't in class. As a matter of fact, he's listed as absent today. Are you sure he isn't in bed with the flu?"

The secretary seemed very contrite. Mrs. Akamasu stood, straightened her skirt, and smiled sadly. "Thank you so much," she said softly and left.

She didn't know where he was. He was supposed to

be in school. It was the best school and even he needed perfect test scores in order to be accepted at Tokyo University when he graduated. No other university was nearly good enough and Genshiro knew it. Unfortunately Genshiro also knew that he would get a perfect score, and without any trouble.

His analytic ability coupled with a photographic memory practically guaranteed that he could pass all the right tests and do all the right things without spending the usual hours at school during the day and in cram school at night, to say nothing of mountains of homework. All Genshiro ever had to do was look over the work and show up for the tests.

A very long time ago Mrs. Akamasu thought of Gen's gifts as a blessing. In the past two years she wasn't sure if they weren't a curse. The hours he didn't need to study were spent away from home, and she didn't know where he went. He had grown his hair long the year before and had put up strange and disturbing posters all over his room. When he was home he lived with headphones on, and he wasn't home very much.

She had to find him now, before his father came home. The letter was in her purse. She had read it over twice, a skinny letter that promised Genshiro a place in the UN Mars program. Well, acceptance into the final testing stage anyway. But Gen always passed tests easily, and so what it really meant was that he was going. She had no doubts at all. But she had to find him and tell him and get him to accept all on his own before he and his father had another fight.

She shook her head and tried to concentrate on the task at hand. She had gone into Gen's evil-looking den, gone through his drawers to find his phone book. She had tried very hard to ignore the ticket stubs she had found, the tapes that had been expressly forbidden in the house. Most of all she tried not to see the handwritten piles of sheet music on the floor.

Not seeing them, she had tucked them under the bed so that her husband wouldn't see. It had been hard.

Going through the phone book had been harder. She didn't recognize most of the names and many of the addresses, and they were in parts of Tokyo that she didn't know. Although she had lived in the city all her life, there were many districts Mrs. Akamasu had never seen. Nor did she want to. Many of the addresses in the book looked like those.

There were girls' names, too, even though the Peer's School did not admit females. At least three of the names in the book she recognized as *gaijen,* not Japanese, although she couldn't tell their nationality.

One phone number was familiar. She studied the name that went with it. Kazuo Ito. She had heard that name before too. Whenever Gen went out, he insisted that he was going to visit his friend Kazuo and had given her that number.

That was where she would start. Not with a phone call, because it was too easy to hide from the phone. No, she would get into a taxi and go to Kazuo's house. If she could find the area. The streets of Tokyo are an unnamed maze, and unless she could find a driver who knew the area, there was no hope.

Resolutely Mrs. Akamasu hailed a cab. The first driver didn't know the address. Neither did the second. It was getting late and she was worried. She stopped two more taxis before she found one that could take her where she needed to go. As the cab crawled through the

33

traffic, she repeated a prayer to herself that Genshiro would be there, that she could bring him home and that he would be pleased.

The ride was long and expensive. The taxi let her off in a seedy neighborhood in front of a poorly kept house. Even from the sidewalk she could hear the howl of electric guitars from the basement. It sounded to her like demons chained in the earth screaming to be freed.

She knocked. The sound was drowned out by the music. Or at least she supposed it was music. She knocked again before she saw the buzzer. She kept the buzzer pressed until the door opened.

A thin girl in tight blue jeans and a little black top stood in the doorway. The girl was smoking a cigarette and Mrs. Akamasu turned her face in distaste. "Is Genshiro Akamasu here?" she asked.

She didn't know what she hoped the answer would be. Much as she wanted to find Gen, and quickly, she didn't want him to be in this house with this girl.

"Yeah," the girl said. "I don't know if he wants to see you, though. They're practicing now."

Mrs. Akamasu had had enough. She was not the granddaughter of Count Toranaka for nothing. She didn't even have to push the girl aside physically; her imperious manner and assumption of propriety swept her past this guardian of the door and down the basement steps.

Genshiro did not see her arrive at first. He was concentrating on the fury he was creating on the drums, borrowed drums that he could use only during stolen hours. The music ripped through him, filled him up, made him safe. When he was playing he wasn't any different from anyone else. He wasn't the star pupil in the entire Peer's School, he wasn't the boy wonder, he wasn't the science nerd that *they* all seemed to think he should be.

And he loved being the rebel. He loved it when someone on the street made some remark about "those bad rocker kids who'll never be anything," knowing that he was destined to join the ranks of the best and brightest. He loved it when he appeared on the math league team in his leathers and long, flying hair, and proceeded to shred the opposition, to solve problems before the moderator had even finishing posing the question. No matter where he was or what anyone expected, he was a shock, and it was the shock he enjoyed most.

This time, though, his mother had turned the tables and it was her turn to shock him. He didn't even think to question how she had found him. It seemed inevitable.

The music faded abruptly. The last resonance of the snare died as the group watched Mrs. Akamasu. Both sides hesitated, power balanced, and then Mrs. Akamasu spoke clearly. "Genshiro, I have some important news for you. Something private."

She turned and left. Gen followed. There was nothing else he could do. He could feel the eyes of the others on him as he climbed the basement stairs. All of them knew that this day would eventually come and that he'd never be back.

When they were out on the street his mother produced the letter, wordlessly laid it across his upturned palm. Genshiro saw the tattered edge, knew that she had opened it, but was too confused and curious to be angry. He didn't have to read it to know that he'd been

35

accepted, but he read it anyway. It bought him time to make a decision.

Genshiro Akamasu had never really figured out if he planned to go through with the whole Mars thing. He had applied more to show that he could, to confront the UN testers with his unquestioned ability and his rock-and-roll rebellion.

He had also been desperately curious. Curious about getting in, curious about what exactly he would have to know, curious about Mars itself. The idea of running off there, to some future that was even more radical than he could have dreamed, appealed to him. Not that Gen had ever admitted to his curiosity aloud. Sometimes he was afraid of just how strong it could be, the crazy obsession to *know*.

"Is this another one of your games, Genshiro?" his mother asked.

The words weren't there again. He had never been very good with words. Music was better. On the drums he could bang out his need, his consuming desire to go "out there." He had never expressed this desire to anyone because it was too tender to expose. Now, suddenly, he was afraid. The whole dream was so very close that he could taste it, and it hung on a very thin string.

He couldn't say it, couldn't twist his tongue around the sounds. And so he just looked at her, silent, hoping that she understood and knowing that she couldn't.

And like a miracle the calm around her evaporated like the morning fog and her face shone brightly. She raised one elegant finger and touched his cheek. "I'll miss you," she said softly.

Her impossible understanding washed over him and made his heart burst with joy. He didn't know that he

36

was crying.

USA: Lanie

The May night was too warm for the black leather
jacket but she wore it anyway. It was one of the few
things she had, and if she was going to get away, she
wasn't going to leave that jacket behind. It represented
too many hours at Frank's Pizza and Subs, too many
nights out on the street waiting for a place that was
warm. She walked down Grange Street, and it sparkled
where the streetlights reflected off the shards of glass in
the gutter. Paper bags blew over the pavement, and
there was the sound of laughter and a boom box over
on the project's playground.

She wasn't going to the playground tonight. And
maybe they wouldn't miss her. Darcy, who had been
her best friend since second grade, had disappeared in
early March. She hadn't said where she was headed,
but Lanie had the idea that she had run away to California, what they'd always talked about. All those summer afternoons sitting on the bench down by the
fountain, she and Darcy had made up stories about
California. When they would go and how they would
get there, and what they would do when they arrived.
Darcy always said that she was going to get a job in a
clothing store and paint T-shirts and eventually become
a designer. But it had been two months and Lanie
hadn't heard anything at all. Maybe Darcy had made it
and the letter hadn't. More likely Darcy was looking for
a place to stay, a good place, so Lanie could come out
and join her.

Anything was better than the projects. She would
join Darcy in a big apartment, where they would have

two cats and all their tapes and Lanie would get a computer. That had been her plan. At school, even with the machines locked up almost all the time, Lanie could get the computer to do whatever she wanted. She had managed to give herself a couple of extra A's in history, her worst subject, and made sure that Darcy and Ed passed.

Made sure Cindy Rizzo passed too. And now it was time to collect.

Cindy Rizzo was not the kind of person Lanie would usually know. Cindy came from the other end of town where the houses were all big and expensive and had swimming pools in the back. Where parents were lawyers and doctors and businesspeople and the kids were in honors classes and expected to go to the best colleges. Cindy Rizzo had everything Lanie had ever wanted. Two parents who lived together and didn't fight all the time, who both worked instead of getting drunk or collecting welfare. Cindy had a room of her own and a phone and her own computer. Cindy also had a real problem with math.

And that's where Lanie came in. Even the teachers, who would never put Lanie in a class with a kid like Cindy, had to admit that the tough-talking street kid from the projects had a gift. First it was math and then it was computers. Lanie could make a computer do anything.

Putting her machines through their paces was the one time she felt good about herself, about the world. For those moments she was the best, she was flying. She didn't have to defer to anyone because they had more money or nicer clothes. Lanie was in control when her hands were on the keyboard and her eyes were on the screen. She could do anything. Anything at all.

Mostly she had messed around with school records to her friends' benefit. A lot of the kids knew it, and no one could trace anything to her. Which is how Cindy got to hear about her. Cindy's folks had promised her a car for her sixteenth birthday as long as she brought home straight A's all year. And thanks to Lanie she had, and a brand-new white CXR was now parked in the driveway.

The deal had been fair. Lanie waited on the corner of Grange and Franklin for the number 27 bus that would take her across town. It wheezed to a stop and she got on. The other people on the bus were old and tired. They probably worked over at Oak Meadow, on their way to the late shift at the country club or back from a day off for the live-in maids. They gave Lanie the creeps. Her mother had once been one of those women, and according to her high school counselor she was next in line. No matter what her abilities, her goals, Lanie came from the projects and had one arrest for shoplifting on her record. The counselor said that no college would take her.

Lanie halfway believed that. She didn't know anyone who had ever been to college, except her teachers, of course. And they all said that with her gift for computers she might want to take a one-year programming course and get a good job.

That made Lanie so angry that she had thrown her books out the window in rage. Because she wasn't from a rich family, because she wore a black leather jacket and bleached her hair blond and hung around with Ed Lantry, she wasn't good enough to use the brain she had. And she knew she had more brain power than most people. Certainly more than Cindy. And now she was going to prove it.

She'd heard about the To Mars Together program at school. It was listed on the computer bulletin board she checked every morning, and there was plenty of talk at the Young Astronauts Club after school. Not that she always went to the club. The teacher didn't see her as a potential Sally Ride. But Lanie knew, she *knew* that she had it.

And the idea had been beautiful, so beautiful that she couldn't believe at first it was real. To go to Mars and start a new world. A place where she could be the person she was without all the labels from the projects and all the troubles at home. To do something that mattered, to run away farther than California and be really free.

She always believed there was another person inside, another Lanie. That other one was smart and kind and capable, someone people respected and who did important things. Someone who did well in life. That was a fantasy Lanie, and she knew it, and she was sure that there would never be a chance to find out if that person was real. Until she had heard about the Mars project.

The bus bumped along where the winter potholes still hadn't been filled in, past the Greyhound station and the Burger King. The air was sweet with spring lilac. Lanie wondered what the air would smell like in a dome on Mars. She blinked hard.

So she had traded with Cindy. Grades and one car for a chance. They had used Cindy's address and recommendations. Cindy had done all the psych counseling and had shared some of the tests with Lanie. That was important. Lanie was no good in history either and had never taken a foreign language, and language was a requirement. Then Lanie had processed it all through the school's best terminal that sat on Mrs. Fillipo's desk. She had created a new record under the name Lanie Rizzo. Her new name. She said it over twice to herself as the bus stopped in front of Whylie's Superette before crossing into Grover Green.

At each stage of the application process she had held her breath, sure it was all over. Pretending that it didn't matter at all to her, that she would just clean out her mother's purse and take the Greyhound to California. The fear was eating at her. For the past few days she hadn't hung out at the playground. She guessed her friends figured she had something else to do. Maybe something to do with Darcy or Ed. It was a good thing that Ed was in the youth reform facility, because she didn't want to face leaving him. All week she hadn't been able to eat. The forms had said May. And it had been May for days and days.

Then Cindy had called after school and left a message. The letter had come. Lanie should come by after dinner, when Cindy's parents were off at their bridge game. Lanie hated the waiting, and all of it because Cindy was too ashamed to introduce her to her parents. It was rotten.

If only, if only things would go right, then she would never have to think about the rotten world again. She would be with others who understood her mind and didn't hate her for being from the Grange Housing Development. Young people who wanted to build a whole new world, a better world, where no one was poor and no parents hit their kids and no one stole cars and ended up in the youth reform facility because it was

41

expected. Where people didn't assume you were a bad kid because you were from the projects.

She nearly missed her stop on the corner of Oak and Madison. The two blocks to Cindy's were very long, the houses all set on oversize lawns. Lanie hated walking in this neighborhood. Once in February she'd been questioned by the police as to her business in the area. They hadn't seemed very convinced that she had a school friend here.

Cindy's house was dark when she walked up the long driveway. She rang the bell into silence and waited. A police patrol car drove by and Lanie shuddered. Finally Cindy came to the door.

Cindy's eyes were red and her face was pinched. She didn't invite Lanie in. "You should have come around the back," she said. "If my folks find out . . ."

Lanie shrugged. There wasn't anything she could do now. Cindy shoved the letter at her as if it were diseased. "Here. Take your letter and get out of here."

"Don't you want to see if we got in?" Lanie asked, ripping the heavy paper.

"What I want is for you to go. My mother saw that letter and asked me about it. And I told her that you couldn't get mail where you live and so I took it for you. My mother saw the letter and called your mother, and she found out that I was lying. You wouldn't believe how mad my parents were. So I've got the car. Big deal. I'm grounded for a month. For telling lies."

Lanie didn't hear a word. She almost couldn't read the letter. Her eyes kept misting over and racing through the crucial paragraph as if she didn't want to know. And then a single word on the second line came into focus. *Accepted* . . . She concentrated and read carefully before she jumped on Cindy's doorstep.

"I made it. We made it. I'm in!" she yelled, throwing her arms around Cindy's neck.

Cindy snorted and stepped outside. "Just promise you won't come back here ever again. I mean that. Ever."

Lanie just smiled. "Don't worry. It's too far to come from Mars just to bother you."

Part II: September

Chapter Four

Houston was hot in September. Nathan thought about all the earlier autumns in his life, returning to school with his friends and the crisp chill in the air. Houston was more like the worst part of summer. And here he was all alone with about a million strange kids milling around.

There had been a bus at the airport specially designated for the Mars group, and the people on it had been a real assortment. Nathan had his skateboard tucked under his arm and was wearing a Powell shirt; some of the guys were dressed in jackets and ties and a few of the girls wore heels. He'd seen at least two school uniforms so far, but he couldn't recognize them.

On the bus there hadn't been much chatter. Everyone was hanging out the windows, wondering if they had arrived yet and what it would be like. No mistake when they got there. Out front, parked on a bank of grass to the right of the entrance, was a Saturn V rocket, disassembled in all its stages.

"That's a real one, too," someone said in a hushed voice behind him.

"The Saturn Five was used for various American space programs, including the Apollo missions. It is a three-stage launch vehicle, 363 feet high and weighs 6,220,000 pounds . . ." It was an Oriental girl wearing dark glasses who was talking—until she was interrupted.

"No one's here to take notes now, so you don't get any points," a girl in a leather jacket said. "And you're not impressing any of us, because we're just as good as you, Miss Teacher's Pet."

"That's why I'm going to Mars and you're not," the Oriental girl replied coldly. Then she folded a stick of chewing gum into her mouth without offering any to anyone else.

Nathan cringed. They hadn't even gotten off the bus yet and the competition was under way. And the Oriental girl looked like one very determined customer.

"Who cares?" a blond male in the back shouted out in thickly accented English. "It is obsolete. Old. No good anymore. We have better rockets. The Proton booster is more powerful."

A chorus of boos greeted that pronouncement, but before anything more could happen the bus stopped in the parking lot and the doors opened. Fifty-two potential Mars explorers stepped out onto the blazing macadam and huddled together, hoping someone would come and rescue them. Nathan stepped a little apart from the group, put his skateboard on the ground, and began a series of half turns around the maze of vehicles. Nothing fancy. But he was concentrating hard enough so that he didn't hear the first announcement, or the second. By the time he got back to the bus, the whole group was already heading toward the white two-story

46

complex that was the main campus of NASA Houston Control. He flipped up his skateboard and ran after them, completely forgetting about his suitcases still in the bus.

"This is the administrative center as well as the research core of the space center," a tall black man was saying, gesturing at the neat rectangle of buildings around a narrow pool. "You won't be spending much time here. As a matter of fact, the less the better. Mission Control is in the building over there, and you will be spending a certain amount of time there. As you may or may not know, working procedure both for NASA and the Soviet programs has been for astronauts to be the primary communicators to any astronaut in space. The job is called capcom, and some of you who are not selected for the first Mars group will be offered this position during the mission.

"And that's right, I said the first group. After the first group establishes the environment, which we expect to take twenty years at least, we expect to see groups going perhaps every ten or so years. Mars is a big place."

"What's going on?" Nathan asked the blond boy with the accent.

"Tour of all the places we won't see again," he replied. "We'll meet our luggage at the dorm and then—here, what is this?"

He handed a sheet of printout to Nathan, who noted the schedule. "Oh, right. Meeting in the theater at five." The blond boy looked blank. "That's seventeen hundred to you, I guess. Where're you from?"

"Leningrad," the blond boy said. "My name is Sergei. Hello."

"Nathan. Hi."

47

They had dropped behind again. Nathan and Sergei jogged to catch up. Nathan found himself breathing hard and sweating through his shirt. And it was September already.

"We won't go any farther until after four, when the tourists have gone. We certainly don't want you kids to become the newest attraction at the center. So we rendezvous at four at the theater. This is the dorm, and you should find your bags in the TV room. I think it's divided boys on the right and girls on the left, but the dorm supervisors will be there to make sure you find your way around. And if you need anything, I'm Lawrence Thompson."

The tall man left them in front of another white building. This one was farther out, though, and was seven stories tall. The TV room was jammed with luggage of all description and people poking at whatever they could find.

"Why don't we find our rooms first and then get our stuff?" Nathan yelled out at the whole crowd.

Someone looked up and made a face. "So who made you boss?"

Nathan shrugged and walked out. At the desk he found the dorm supervisors weren't the iron maidens of school secretarydom, but people who looked only a little older than themselves. They all held clipboards with lists that looked suspiciously like summer camp.

"Nathan Long? Yes, here. Three fifty-seven. You're with Chuvakin," the resident assistant said. He looked like a student teacher Nathan had had in gym a few years earlier.

The blond boy with the accent smiled. "That's me. So fate seems to take a hand."

"Fine with me. I figured you for one okay guy when I saw you try to get those girls on the bus to stop playing Can You Top This," Nathan said.

They found the room, a plain, rectangular room with beds, desk, chairs, and lamps. Nothing at all personal anywhere. Nathan lay his skateboard on one of the beds, claiming it and that side of the room. "And where's the computer?" Nathan asked the walls. "I mean, how are we supposed to live without a computer?"

"You didn't expect them to give us a computer in each room?" Sergei asked with amazement.

"No, I sure didn't," Nathan replied. "I expected that we'd each get our own. How else are we going to do anything?"

Sergei whistled through his teeth. "Well, maybe the mob has cleared out of the TV room now and we can get our things."

They returned to a scene of chaos. People were hauling suitcases over each other, banging and crawling through the mess to try to find their own bags. Sergei located his trunk and he and Nathan hauled it upstairs before going for the rest of their gear. By the time they got to the room, it was time to head over to the theater.

The theater reminded Nathan of an old-style movie theater, down to the plush seats and the giant five-story screen. "For IMAX movies," the girl who seemed so sure of herself said. "There are at least three places where they are shown in this country—here, the Smithsonian, and the Kennedy Space Center at Cape Canaveral."

"Will someone shut her up? Or use her chewing gum to paste her mouth shut?" a boy behind Nathan mut-

49

tered. He agreed with the sentiment.

They'd all been waiting so long, that was the problem, Nathan thought. Like on the first day of school. There really isn't anything to do, and he couldn't help getting bored and anxious at the same time. And then the lights dimmed only the smallest amount and four people got up on the tiny platform before the screen. One of them Nathan recognized as Lawrence Thompson.

It was an older woman, though, who got up to the podium. A hush settled on the auditorium. The woman looked them over and seemed pleased.

"Excellent," she said softly. "First, let me welcome you on behalf of the United Nations to the Houston Space Center and the To Mars Together program. Never in the history of our species have we gathered together so many bright, promising, and hardworking young people from so many places on our planet. That's only the first first. All of you are exceptional or you wouldn't be here. There isn't a single one of you who hasn't shown intelligence, determination, and character. Any of you would make fine candidates as pioneers.

"Which is why we have this final selection process, to get to know all of you personally over a period of time. Unfortunately, there are only four hundred places in our three first ships, and so it is not possible for us to send all of you. Remember, you are not only competing against the others here in Houston, but at our programs in Star City, Geneva, and New Delhi as well.

"Let me introduce my colleagues to you. I am Dr. Eileen Gardner, in charge of astronaut training programs. I will not be coming to Mars with you, and that is the greatest sorrow in my life. These three people" —

50

she gestured to those sitting behind her — "will have that honor. They are all specialists with skills necessary to the new colony, skills that we cannot teach in a year or two, let alone the six months before launch. They are also your astronaut advisers, both scholastic and personal. Each one of them is a qualified astronaut as well as a specialist in a scientific discipline, and they have some training in personal counseling as well. We urge you to get to know them and use their expertise. They are here to help you.

"Dr. Martin Gold is an astronaut-geologist, Dr. Mary Elizabeth Allen is an astronaut-physician, and Dr. Lawrence Thompson is an astronaut-physicist.

"Aside from introductions, I must point out again that humanity has never taken a true step in living away from Earth. You will be the first. And as such, we have decided to gear this final phase of selection in a new and innovative way. Each of you will be assigned to teams. The lists are being passed out now, so you will be able to meet the rest of your team over dinner. Teams will either succeed together or fail together. There will be no transfers permitted for any reason. How you work as a team is one of the most important aspects of this phase of this process. All for one and one for all. You will be expected to elect a team leader by January first, and you will be notified shortly thereafter as to which teams will be going on to that greatest of all adventures — Mars.

"Your program will consist of several different challenges. There will be classes, naturally, not only in chemistry, astronomy, physics, celestial mechanics, and astronautics, but in agronomy and engineering. You will be expected to follow a vigorous physical fitness regimen as well. We can't afford to send anyone who can't stand the physical stress of setting up a new colony. And, finally, to pull it all together, each team will compete in a survival trek that will utilize your physical and intellectual skills and test your ability to work together.

"It will be a busy and, I hope, rewarding time for all of you. Remember, never in the history of the human race has anyone tried anything so daring and with so much promise. Mars will shape you as you will shape it. One day its red land will be your only real home. The night sky will look naked and strange without two moons. And until several generations of terraforming have created real oceans, there is a good chance that none of you will ever go out for a surfing championship or design bikinis."

The polite laughter was just a little nervous as well. "No girls in bikinis?" Sergei whispered. "The sacrifices demanded by science!"

The speaker waited for the laughter to die down. "And as an introduction to your destination, we have several pictures from a recent fly-by.

"Mars is the fourth planet in our solar system, but only by default. It lies past an asteroid belt that was once believed to be all that remained of a planet shattered upon impact with some giant object. Perhaps it was the same object that some people theorize might have knocked Earth onto its axis and gave us seasons. The same process may have happened to Mars, since it, too, has a tilted axis and seasons. We can see that from the way the ice caps expand and retreat at regular intervals. The asteroid belt may also have been a protoplanet—of a planet that never formed.

"Mars is much smaller than Earth, with a diameter of 4,222 miles, which means that it has far less mass. And less mass, as you know, indicates less gravity. In fact, Mars has only a third the gravity Earth does. And even though it is so much smaller, its day is twenty-four hours, thirty-nine minutes and twenty-three seconds, which is so close to ours that it's almost spooky.

"The famous ice caps are mainly frozen carbon dioxide, but there is a trace of water vapor in the atmosphere. Not much, certainly not as much as Earth with our vast oceans. In fact, for Mars to be made fully habitable, oceans will have to be created. But the presence of water already shows us that the surface has at least several Earthlike qualities that will make your mission possible. The famous canals of Mars were once believed to have been great waterways although we now know this is not true. The surface is also marked with dormant volcanoes, which indicate the potential for an Earthlike habitation.

"Without the volcanic activity denoting a molten core, Mars would be far too cold to colonize, as it is 141 million miles from the sun, in contrast to the 93 million miles that Earth is from the sun. That also makes the year almost twice as long. Six hundred eighty-seven days instead of three hundred sixty-five.

"But enough talk. Let's see the pictures."

The theater darkened and the giant screen filled with glowing red. The surface of Mars was almost as he had imagined it, Nathan thought with awe. A starkly beautiful desert, the landscape was rich with mountains and craters. From this angle he couldn't see the famed ice caps, but just the knowledge of their existence chilled him. So very silent and empty, so very far away. Nathan wondered if Columbus thought of that when he set out from Spain.

No, Columbus thought he was headed to India. He couldn't have known, have seen so clearly. Something about seeing the red planet in this place made him desire it as he had never thought possible. Nathan Long had thought that he had come only to get to college. He had never expected to fall in love with Mars.

When they emerged back into the sunlit Houston afternoon, Nathan was disoriented. For a moment he had forgotten where he was and why he held the paper in his hands. The paper was a printout list of his team. At the top was the name, Long, in extra-large letters. He scanned the list but none of the names meant anything to him.

"You are Long, Nathan?" a girl's sharp voice cut into his musings. He looked up from the paper. It was the know-it-all from the bus. From the way she looked at him now, Nathan decided that he had never in his life met anyone so stuck-up.

"Yeah," he said, meeting her challenging tone.

"You took the wrong list," she said, waving a green and white striped sheet in accusation. "This is Long, Nathan."

Nathan looked at his printout again. The Long was written out in very large letters. The name *Oh Suk* was beneath the *Long* and in rather small type. He had been so involved in Mars that he hadn't noticed.

"Sorry," Nathan said coldly as they exchanged lists.

The girl shuddered delicately as they made the exchange and then looked coldly into his face. "You are precisely the kind of person I came here to get away from. The kind who make mistakes. I'm glad you're not on *my* team." Then she turned her back and walked away.

What a little snob, he thought. He was too shocked by her rudeness and self-important manner to be angry at first. Who did she think she was? They might have the same last name, but that was all they had in common, and Nathan was very glad that they couldn't possibly be related.

Well, he wasn't going to let one miserable snob bother him, he decided. He read through the names on his list and tried to put faces to them. These people were going to either make his dream or stand in his way. They counted.

Genshiro Akamasu was the first name, and when Nathan realized it was Japanese, he groaned. He had heard stories of Japanese students all being super competitive and real grinds. No fun at all. Sergei Chuvakin was next, and Nathan smiled. That must have been why they had been assigned as roommates. And he already knew the Russian kid was the kind of person he wanted on his side. Then came Karl Muller of Germany, Lanie Rizzo, who was American, Alice Thorne from New Zealand, and Noemi Velazquez from Venezuela. At the bottom was the information that dinner started at six P.M. and his team was assigned to table twenty-nine.

It was already five-thirty, and from the map posted outside the theater he could see that the dining hall was on the other side of the center. Might as well get over there now and meet his team.

Chapter Five

The food in the cafeteria line was singularly unappealing. Limp broccoli and rice and a yellow squash casserole, or something labeled chicken Tetrazzini. Nathan had had too many bad experiences with that dish to risk it. He retreated to the sandwich line, which wasn't much better. But at least the peanut butter was recognizable. He made three sandwiches and went to table twenty-nine.

Four people were there already, and three of them had sandwiches on their trays. "I don't know what that yellow stuff is," one of the girls was saying, "but it reminds me of the hospital. You know, everything very nutritious and horrible."

From his list Nathan decided that the boy who looked like a Japanese version of Bon Jovi had to be Genshiro Akamasu. Nathan was very surprised. He'd thought that all Japanese students were squares and nerds. With hair down to his shoulders and a silver earring, this Genshiro certainly didn't look like the eager-beaver type. On the other hand, he was the one who didn't have a sandwich—he had three bowls of plain rice. And he was poking one of them as if it might contain hidden cockroaches.

"Now we know how the selection process works," said the girl who had spoken before. She had long braids and a broad accent that Nathan couldn't place. Not quite Aussie, he thought, but not really English either. He tried to think of other countries where they spoke English. South Africa, maybe. And then he remembered the list. New Zealand.

She wasn't pretty, he thought, and wondered if Sergei would be disappointed. The only color he knew to call her hair was dishwater brown, and her face was broad and ruddy. "Healthy" would be the best way to describe her.

Genshiro laughed. "Right. We all eat, and whoever doesn't die goes."

"I'm Alice," the girl with braids said. "And this is Lanie." She gestured at a girl with bleached-blond hair and a cocky expression. She was cute, Nathan thought, but he was a little put off by the tough way she dressed. "Who are you?" Alice asked.

"Nathan Long."

Genshiro said they should call him Gen, and he introduced the other boy as his roommate, Karl Muller. The German boy was pure prep as far as Nathan could figure. With his nice slacks, short haircut, and perfectly shined shoes, he was every teacher's dream. He might not be good-looking enough to give Sergei any real competition, but Nathan knew that a lot of girls went for Karl's type. For some reason Karl looked perfectly miserable and said nothing. Nathan decided it was probably due to the lack of decent food. He was not all that happy himself about facing months of lousy food.

No way, he told himself. It's just the first night. It's got to get better.

Just then Sergei appeared at his elbow with an amazingly beautiful brunette dressed in a black miniskirt with hot pink suspenders over a white blouse. Her fingernails were the same color as the suspenders and her heels were at least three inches high, Nathan figured. Sergei caught Nathan's eye and waggled his eyebrows to express his satisfaction with this particular member. She was a looker. In fact, everyone seemed pleased to see them except Karl, who looked at the girl's impractical shoes with disgust.

"Sergei! Isn't it great? We're on the same team!" Nathan said, smiling.

"That's probably why we're roommates," Sergei said. "This is Noemi. She's also on our list."

"Hey, Noemi," Alice asked. "Why'd you take that yellow glop?"

Noemi smiled. "It looks very low calorie, don't you think?" she chattered, taking a seat next to Lanie.

"Looks like the girls all know each other already," Sergei said.

"Well, we're all roommates," Noemi said.

"I wish I could transfer out of this group," Karl said, his first statement of the evening.

"Well, you can't," Lanie told him sharply. "You're stuck with us."

"It's just a little early yet to decide something like that," Nathan said, trying to smile. "How about waiting until you get to know people?"

Karl looked down at his plate. It had half a ham sandwich, the same thing Sergei had gotten and Nathan had avoided. The ham had looked pressed and processed, just like the turkey, and he was sure it had no flavor. At least they couldn't ruin peanut butter that had come in a comfortingly familiar Skippy jar. Just like home.

"Before you complain about your assignment, maybe we should find something to eat." Lanic spoke for the first time. "If anyone had any money, we could call out for Domino's."

Nathan smiled. "With sausage and onions? Let's do it."

"Domino's doesn't deliver on Mars," Alice pointed out quite unhappily.

"We shouldn't even be talking about food. We should be talking about strategy, about how we're going to combine our abilities to win. Not something stupid like pizza," Karl said.

Nathan wanted to say something to calm Karl down. The guy hadn't even given them a chance. "Look, we can all decide right here and now that we can't stand each other and we're going to fail. But I for one really want to go to Mars. More than anything. And for me to go, I've got to be part of a team that's going. Those are the rules. So we all have to agree that we're going to go all out, or else we might as well go home now."

"And it's a stupid rule. It stinks," Karl argued, his eyes flashing. "I should be able to make the selection on my own merits, not have to worry about the intelligence of a person who looks like she never read anything more demanding than a fashion magazine. What do you plan to do? Design space suits with little flower prints on them?" he asked Noemi, who looked shocked at this unexpected attack.

Lanie's mouth turned up in a sneer and her nostrils

59

flared. "And what did we do to be so lucky to get you?" she asked, her voice heavy with anger. "I know your type, rich-boy bonehead thinks all the girls are just waiting by the phone. Well, you can stuff it, rich boy."

"Hey, look, you two are making this dinner even worse. And I didn't think it could get any worse," Nathan tried to joke.

But Sergei had already cut in. "Hey, wait a minute. Let's go back to pizza. Pizza is not stupid. Food is maybe the most important thing there is, the most important thing for anyone planning to build a new world."

"Well, oxygen and water might come first," Nathan added.

Sergei shook his head. "Growing plants, food, *makes* oxygen. That's how we'll create an atmosphere. And oxygen and hydrogen together make water, so we'll have that too. But the plants are essential, and we eat the plants, so they serve two purposes."

"I didn't come here to be a farmer," Karl said angrily. "I'm a scientist. I'm going to be a scientist."

Alice's face flushed deep red. "Well, my parents are farmers. And they know ten times more genetics and soil chemistry and biology than any university genius who's too good to get his hands dirty. Mendel discovered genetics when he was growing flowers, so there! Not in some lab."

Nathan felt sorry for Alice. Her blue eyes were full of tears, and she twisted one long heavy braid around her fingers. He had automatically trusted Alice as a teammate. She would be no problem. But Karl was a real troublemaker. He really did seem too stuck-up to do them any good. And he wondered about the others as well. Glancing over his own team, he thought they surely didn't look like a bunch of brains. Noemi was filing her long nails and Lanie was huddled into her leather jacket even though it was seventy degrees out. Gen was staring into space, ignoring the conversation, as if he were on some kind of high. On the other hand, Nathan knew that he didn't exactly look like a stereotypical "brain" himself.

"Hey, remember what they said." Nathan interrupted what seemed a bad argument in the making. "We either make it as a team or we fail as a team. As a team, get it? So, like Benjamin Franklin said, we'd better hang together or else we're really gonna hang separately."

"The desserts looked pretty good," Sergei said, changing the subject. "And if I don't get something decent to eat, I'm going to die of starvation before we ever get close to a rocket."

Lanie and Noemi joined him on the line. The three of them returned with a tray full of ice cream, chocolate pudding, spice cake, and giant-size soft cookies. Alice passed the largest piece of cake over to Karl, a peace offering, Nathan suspected, and the group pretended that everything was fine.

That night Nathan couldn't sleep. After dinner he and Sergei had returned to their room to unpack and settle in. Now the humid warmth smelled of night and the sheets were too stiff and new for him to feel comfortable. It had been a long day. By rights he should have been very tired. But he couldn't help thinking about how they were going to make the team work.

There wasn't any choice. If Karl kept on being a jerk,

61

it messed up everything for all of them. And he wanted to go to Mars. He could taste the desire. A whole new world, a new start. No war, no pollution, nobody locking anyone else up because they didn't like the leaders. No hunger, no illiteracy, no one rich while someone else was poor. No one whose mom had to work as a word processor because it was less of a risk than owning the flower shop she had always wanted.

Nathan wondered if now that he was gone, taken care of, she would go down to the bank and apply for a loan. Somehow that thought stuck in his throat and made it hard to breathe.

"You up?" Sergei whispered from across the room.

"You too?" Nathan answered. "We got an early day tomorrow."

"I'm worried about Karl."

"Me too," Nathan replied, glad to have this excuse for feeling out of sorts. "But what can we do to straighten the guy out?" He hesitated, aware of the strangeness of the Houston night. "You know, I'm still hungry. Did you notice a snack machine in the TV lounge?"

"Absolutely," Sergei replied, happiness in the whisper. "Exactly what I was thinking. I can't sleep on an empty stomach."

"Bad dreams," Nathan agreed. He switched on the light, pulled on his jeans, and slipped on a blue Space Shuttle T-shirt. Sergei put on his slacks and undershirt and they left the room.

The corridor was quiet and they were barefoot. The cool tile was the only thing Nathan had encountered that wasn't miserably warm. Only a few utility lights pierced the dark, and there were deep shadows around the door frames. An exit sign blinked red in a shadowy

62

corner.

The stairs were even darker than the hall. Nathan wished he'd thought of bringing a flashlight. Next time. He'd have to remember. He clung to the iron rail as he felt his way from one step to the next. He didn't even remember how long the flights were. He had to slide his foot along the edge of the step, searching for the landing.

"That's three flights," Sergei whispered behind him.

Nathan wasn't sure, but he felt around for the door. He found a handle, opened it, walked through, and smashed into a bucket. It made a terrible racket and he groped for the light. A utility closet. The light was blinding.

"Good idea," Sergei whispered. "Over here."

The Russian took over the lead as they came out of the stairwell and found themselves in the lobby. Even without light it wasn't too dark. The large plate-glass doors let in almost enough starlight to read by.

"Look at that," Nathan said, pointing.

From the lobby doors they could see the Milky Way spread across the sky. Stars glittered white against the indigo like diamonds. And, like diamonds, some of them were tinged with red or yellow or blue or violet.

It was as if a magnet had drawn Nathan outside. He didn't even hear the door lock behind him as he wandered down the two decorative steps and out onto the well-tended lawn. His hunger was forgotten as he feasted on the glory of the stars overhead.

He could pick out Vega, the white star that was the second most brilliant visible in the Northern Hemisphere. From Vega he could find Deneb and Altair. And finding Deneb, he could trace the Coal Sack, a

63

dark area of the Milky Way created by cosmic dust and not lit by any nearby stars. It was magnificent.

"Look," Serge said in a hushed voice, pointing. "In Andromeda. There's M31. The Great Nebula."

Nathan followed his finger. Faint in the rich field of stars he could see the light and swallowed hard. The very photons that told his eyes that light was there had come from another galaxy. It was the only other galaxy visible to the naked eye, and a spiral like the Milky Way. Nathan had seen pictures, but at home with the streetlights and the glitter from the city only six miles off, he had never been able to see it real and live.

His mouth was dry just thinking about it. Light from another galaxy. Someplace humanity could never hope to travel. Something so tantalizing and so very very far. What wonders did they have, he thought, on all those billions of stars that he saw as a single faint glow? What strange beauties were under their alien skies?

"What are you kids doing out?" an angry voice demanded.

Nathan wheeled around. Dr. Thompson stood over them, shaking his head.

"We were just looking at the stars," he said lamely.

"You can't see them like this at home," Sergei added. "There's too much light in the city."

Dr. Thompson just continued to look at them. "You knew this was against the rules. You can't wait even twenty-four hours before you start making trouble, can you? Long and Chuvakin, right? The door to the dorm's locked. How are you planning to get back in, put Spider-Man out of a job?"

Nathan was suddenly ashamed. Before the supervisor had shown up, he had been having a great time.

Now it was all spoiled.

Dr. Thompson's expression went from simply angry to disappointed. "You know you're going to get to look through the big telescopes. It's on the schedule. Unless you didn't bother with that either. Astronomy. Very important component of your training here. You'll see all the stars you can ever imagine. So. How did you plan to get back in?"

"We didn't plan to go out, sir," Sergei said penitently. "We were just up and saw the stars and didn't think about it really."

"And you expect us to be impressed with a couple of kids who can't bother to think about things before they run off? No discipline, no sense at all. And we're supposed to send you off to another planet? I wouldn't send you down the block to buy milk." Thompson practically spat out the words.

He stepped up to the door, then turned to them. "Well, come on. Move it. Before I write you up for insolence as well as for breaking the rules."

He took out a ring thick with keys and selected the proper one, then ushered them both back inside. "You've got early class tomorrow. Due to breakfast by seven. Don't be late."

When he got back into bed Nathan was more worried than angry. Here it was, only the first day, and they already had a bad rep. He had risked his own dreams, and all the others as well. He'd just have to make it up to them. More than make it up. He had seen the pictures of Mars, had seen the stars, and there was nothing in the whole world he would not do to go there. His dreams that night were full of millions of stars and a distant galaxy.

65

Chapter Six

On the second day they began with two hours of gym class. Nathan, with all his skateboarding, thought he was pretty good in the balance department, and Sergei and Gen were good. But Karl was amazing. He could do anything—run, climb, do more chin-ups than anyone else. So Nathan was properly subdued when they got out and swarmed around the bulletin board for the day's scores.

Every day individual scores were posted in every section. "Hey, look, we're pretty hot," Sergei said, pointing to several scores. Nathan was pleased at how well he'd placed in computers, and he was surprised to see that Lanie was ahead of him there. Just as well, since her other scores were all over the place. Except for Karl, all of their scores were like that: highs and lows but nothing consistent. Karl, on the other hand, kept a good strong average in everything. Not a number one or two like Noemi and Gen, but a solid fifteen in almost everything except pure math, where he was a good bit lower.

Well, some people were cut out to be theoretical and some were applied. That was the way the world was.

After the scores were posted, they had a tour of the astronaut training facilities. They saw the immersion tanks, where astronauts practiced weightlessness with the aid of scuba divers. Past the gyros that rotated people on all three axes. Past the hydroponic gardens and the imaging center and the communications consoles. They saw pictures from space, of Earth from space, tried to pick out their own cities from the lights and the rivers.

They were escorted into the labs and shown spectragraphs of different stars, computer-enhanced images that showed both the Earth and the Milky Way in infrared, their heat patterns making a whole different configuration. They saw pictures taken in the bands of radio waves and even got to listen to the background radiation static that permeated the universe. The noise that was the still living echo of the big bang.

"And that's just the astrophysics section," Gen whispered. "Too cool. Bio's tomorrow."

Nathan nodded, but he didn't need to hold out. Since he first glimpsed M31, he knew what he wanted to specialize in. Too bad astrophysics wasn't one of the more important courses for a colonist.

"But it is," Alice had reassured him at lunch. Somehow, with her braids falling almost to her tray and her ancient oversize sweater, she looked almost like a colonist already, so it really meant something that she thought it was important. Especially after the way she had put Karl in his place the night before at dinner. "How else are we going to navigate?"

"It's all so, so *applied*," Noemi said, wringing her hands.

"What is? Lunch?" Gen teased back. "You couldn't

67

apply this lunch to a mile of Super Glue."

Alice had made a face, and Nathan secretly had to agree with her. There wasn't much they could do to mess up cereal and orange juice at breakfast, but lunch was just more glop and sandwiches, and Nathan didn't hold out much hope for dinner.

"The part I liked best was the pictures of Earth," Sergei said when he had finished one of the six apples and three bananas on his plate. "Especially the ones done with radar where they showed the river paths under the Sahara. And the fact that those underground ways are still there and the desert could be made alive. That was the best."

"You're going to specialize in imaging?" Nathan asked.

"No," Sergei said. "At first I thought chemistry. That was what I was best at in school. But geology is getting very interesting. And someone's got to do it for the group. And I don't think Noemi would know a rock if she fell over one."

Noemi giggled and fluttered her fingers. This morning her long nails were bright red. "I wouldn't. So what? I don't know what I want to specialize in. I mean, I always thought I'd do pure math. It's so beautiful, and no one can ever use it to hurt anyone."

"No one can use it at all," Gen said helpfully. "I think that the man who invented matrix multiplication would be miserable if he knew there was a real practical use for his work these days. But we're going to have to choose soon if we're going to place in the games."

"What about you, Karl?" Alice asked. "What are you thinking about doing?"

Karl went on eating his salad and pretended that he

didn't hear her. Alice rolled her eyes in frustration and absently twisted a braid around her hand. Nathan was relieved that for once Noemi didn't giggle.

"You've got to pick something," Lanie insisted, plowing right through the others' helplessness. "I'm doing computers. That's what I was good at in school. It was the only part of school I liked, really. Used to break into the net and change everybody's grades and stuff. That was pretty cool."

"Did you ever break into a bank or a defense installation?" Noemi wanted to know.

Lanie gagged on her Coke. "No. I'd have been caught and put in jail for about a million years if I did that."

"Might have been better," Karl muttered under his breath. "That's where juvenile delinquents belong." Before Lanie could say anything, he looked at Alice and said, "I am going to specialize in the one useful and important thing on this team, which is engineering. Like I always planned to, not that anyone else here could do a decent job."

"Hey, man, like I thought I would do that too," Gen said quickly. "Or biology. I figured that bio would be a big deal in a new environment. Genetic engineering, you know? Create Martian specialties — red rice, super avocados, maybe prespiced guacamole."

Karl looked as if he were going to be sick. Lanie was probably already a criminal, and Noemi didn't seem to care about anything except the color of her nails and trying to get Alice to change that horrible sweater. Not that anything could improve Alice, Karl thought. She was hopeless, a rube of the worst kind, no background in anything important. As for the guys, he wasn't impressed there either. So far as he could see, the Russian was girl crazy, and Gen was just plain weird. And that American, Nathan, he seemed as though all he wanted to do was take over.

"What do you think about this survival trek idea?" Nathan asked, desperate to change the subject. "We get to build or make anything we think we might need. Maybe we should each begin a design for some type of vehicle."

"I would have thought it would make more sense for each of us to work on what we like best," Alice said thoughtfully. "Maybe you could work on a navigation system and I could put together first aid. Maybe the engineers could work on the vehicle."

"Which means you want me to do all the work so that you can win," Karl said angrily. "After Nathan and Sergei already got us into trouble, too. Well, you're not going to make me do all the work."

"No one's asking you to," Noemi said. "Your scores in pure math were merely average."

Karl turned red. Everyone knew that Noemi and Gen had scored one and two on those, and had put the team in the top half academically. But the German boy couldn't resist pointing out that Noemi had also scored dead last in physical fitness. "You can't even jog a mile," he said. "Talk about bringing our score down. You bring it down in physical, Sergei and Nathan here go and get us seventeen demerits our first day here, and Lanie's gonna get arrested for something."

Noemi looked as if she were going to cry. Just the way she had on the track earlier that morning in her pink and green designer sweats. "He's just being a geek, Noemi," Lanie explained, flashing the evil eye at Karl.

70

"Ignore him. I'll work out with you extra. You should like it; it burns calories."

Nathan gave up. He took his tray to the busing window and left the dining hall. He wished it weren't so far to the dorm or he'd get his skateboard. Somehow he could always think better when he was moving, when his body caught a rhythm and had his full attention. Then his mind was free of the false boundaries and his imagination soared. There were no limits, and that was how all his best ideas had come.

But it was too far to get his skateboard and they had another lab introduction in half an hour. So Nathan walked. The white paths gleamed against the lawn in the bright Texas light.

They had to do something. Nathan let his mind wander. He pictured the material he had seen earlier that day in the labs. Someone had given a very short talk on the supernova, just an introduction. How a massive star eats itself alive, and how its own gravity begins to gain against the pressure of the activity. And when it explodes it blows off a cloud of material. The ring nebula was like that. He had once brought pictures to show to his ninth-grade class of a little star surrounded by a perfect smoke ring of debris.

But the best part was that the supernova observed confirmed the theories about how stars collapse. Neutrinos had been observed on Earth eleven hours before the event, just the way the theory had predicted. So it wasn't a theory anymore. It was fact. Theories made predictions about how the real world would act. Nathan liked that statement. Somehow it made him think of the team, and Karl.

The pressure of the team — especially Karl — pushing

out against the gravity, the threat of the other teams, pulled them together.

There had to be something else that would be the gravity, something stronger than the competition of the other groups. Only Nathan couldn't think of what it could be.

The past three hours had seemed like the longest in Nathan's life. Okay, so Karl didn't like Gen's music. Gen brought his tapes over to Nathan and Sergei's room, and his guitar as well.

"He kicked me out," Gen announced as he stepped through their door. "He said if I couldn't study quietly, then I'd better take my music and leave. I mean, you might not like the selection, or maybe you want quiet right then, but you work it out. I'm cool, I'm willing to talk. But when he unplugged my guitar, well, that was it. And I wasn't even playing either."

Sergei was fascinated with the guitar. He'd never held an electric before. "But how does it work?" he kept demanding of every facet Gen showed him. He pulled out the screwdriver attachment on Nathan's Swiss Army knife and began taking off the tremolo arm.

"Wait," Gen said, diving across the room to rescue his prize possession. "Don't do that."

"But I just wanted to see," Sergei apologized.

"It's all microchips, so there isn't anything to see," Gen told him. "You've already taken apart our class terminal and the dishwasher and I've had to put them back together."

"I would have put them back if you hadn't been in such a rush," Sergei protested. "I still say that we had at

72

least another fifteen minutes on the dishwasher."

"Yeah, but we don't need any more demerits," Gen added. "We're already way at the head of the list on those. And maybe you don't mind Dr. Thompson finding you and chewing your tail off, but that isn't exactly my idea of a good time."

Nathan shook his head. After only three days the argument was old. And friendly. Already they were teasing each other, had traditions and special ways of doing things. And even a traditional enemy.

It seemed that Suki Long had decided to hold a grudge against Nathan ever since he had confused their lists on the first day, and she hadn't passed up an opportunity to treat his team nastily ever since. It was kind of fun, actually. So far the best was when Lanie had shot her with vinegar from a water pistol during an after-hours water balloon fight. Naturally, Suki had not been participating. She had been trying to close the fun down. But the vinegar had turned all the silver jewelry she had been wearing black.

"It was Noemi's idea," Lanie said modestly. "I just did the shooting because my aim's pretty good."

It was really funny, everyone agreed, and Suki certainly deserved it. The only problem was that Suki was also a tattle-tale and had gone to Dr. Thompson. The team had gotten twenty demerits for that.

"I don't know why," Sergei had said, staunchly standing up for Noemi and Lanie. "A little practical chemistry. Big deal. It isn't as if a little polish won't take care of everything."

"Who cares about twenty demerits anyway?" Nathan had put on his best attitude. "All for one and one for all, like the book says."

73

"It was stupid and childish," Karl had said. "And when Dr. Thompson asked me to verify the accounts, I agreed."

Lanie had jumped at Karl so quickly that Sergei and Nathan couldn't move quickly enough to restrain her. She managed to scratch Karl's cheek and tear off his glasses before they hauled her off. That's when Karl had gone off, supposedly to the first aid center. But this morning Lanie had five more personal demerits next to her name.

They didn't know what to do about Karl. That was the problem. Here they were, Nathan and Gen and Sergei, all fooling around together, half studying and half going through Gen's tape collection.

Over on the girls' side Nathan knew that Lanie and Alice and Noemi were having a good time. They were tight. The whole team was, except Karl.

But for the past three hours all they could talk about was Karl. Why didn't he like them, and what was his problem anyway? Sergei wondered if maybe he was just too square for them. Secretly Nathan agreed but didn't want to say so. No matter what the reason, they were going to have to live with the guy. Especially Genshiro, who was his roommate.

And so they had begun to hatch a plan. Time was limited and so it wasn't exactly as polished as it could be, and frankly Nathan was more than a little worried that the whole thing could backfire royally. But at this point that wouldn't matter. They were already in serious trouble with a member who was dragging the whole group down. Not only did Karl not do his share in the competition or group housekeeping, his attitude problem made everyone uncomfortable. Things like the water fight that should have been fun were totally ruined.

Therefore, the plan. They'd spent the past half hour on the dorm phone over to the girls' side, mostly talking to Alice. Lanie wanted only to strangle Karl, and Noemi wasn't really great at people skills. Except for the areas where she excelled, she might as well be on Mars already.

Nathan wasn't sure he was ready to break all the rules and get into trouble. The only problem was, they were already in trouble. Getting caught now couldn't possibly make things worse. He kept telling himself that, but his stomach didn't believe it.

"It's ten-thirty," Sergei informed them. "Time to go."

"Are you sure they'll be on time tonight?" Nathan asked. "Maybe we should give them ten more minutes."

"No way," Sergei said. "They said they'd be on time."

Nathan smiled and opened the window. On the third floor the rooms were set back so there was a wide ledge where the second floor ended. Plenty of room to sit, take out the boom box, walk around, and look at the stars. And obey curfew at the same time, since they hadn't left the building.

Out on the ledge, Nathan handed the rope to Sergei and waited. Then he crept down, counting the windows. Two, three, four . . . the one that was open had to be Gen's. Gen and Karl's. Nathan leaned against the wall and pulled himself up under the window and looked in. Karl was sitting hunched over his desk, an open book in front of him. He kept rubbing his eyes.

Very quietly Nathan balanced on the sill and swung his legs into the room. He waited for a moment before he cleared his throat. "Umm, Karl, we had an idea," he

75

said slowly.

Karl jumped and turned, startled at the voice. "I didn't let you in," he protested. He looked as if he were about to kill someone, and the only thing that stopped him was that he couldn't decide if Nathan or Genshiro should be first. Nathan tried to stay relaxed. He didn't want to alarm Karl more than he had already. Only how did he show Karl that they needed to be friends? That none of them would make it unless they all worked together? Karl didn't seem to want to understand that.

"So where's Sergei? Or is he going to pop through the window too?" Karl asked.

Nathan sighed in frustration. "You know, Karl Muller, you are one hard case. I mean it. We thought that a little team exercise was in order. Morale building. Since tomorrow is the first round in the computer races. We thought a little excursion would get us all geared up."

"What we need is a good night's sleep," Karl said angrily. "And plenty of study. Which we don't have the time to do now. And it's after curfew, and if we're caught, we're in trouble."

"Which is why this will build team spirit," Gen chimed in. "We disobey together, we make it through together, we have something special we share."

"Yeah," Karl said. "Secret criminal records."

"Wait a minute." Nathan held his hands in the time-out signal. "There isn't anything criminal about going out to the Hard Rock Cafe. There isn't even anything vaguely bad about it. So there's a rule here that we have to stay in after ten. Big deal. Who's gonna watch the clocks on Mars?"

76

Karl sat down at the desk and pretended to read again. "You're a bunch of stupid kids. None of you is serious about anything. You don't think anything is important. Well, forget it. I'm staying here and studying. And if you all want to get caught playing some dumb trick, it isn't my business."

"I know," Gen said slowly. "You're scared."

Karl's eyes flashed, and he sneered. "If you mean I don't want to be caught and thrown out of the program, you've got it. But afraid to go into town to some club? Like the man says, there isn't even anything vaguely interesting about it."

Gen rested his chin on his fist. "I don't know. I think you're scared that someone's gonna catch mama's good boy breaking the rules. I think you don't even think twice about rules, or if they make sense or not. You're a good little sheep ready to jump off the cliff because that's what good little sheep do. Well, I don't care what the sheep do, and when I read the instruction book I check if it makes sense. You don't think any more than a machine that I can turn on and off. You don't think for yourself at all."

Nathan held his breath. Gen had gone further than they'd agreed, much further. Sergei had been sure that calling him a coward would be enough to do the trick. And Nathan was worried that what Gen had done was dangerous, not just for the evening but for the future of the entire group. It didn't help at all that Nathan agreed with every word he'd said, and Alice was the one who'd pointed it all out in the first place.

What mattered was Karl, who looked ready to explode.

"All right," Karl said softly, rising from the desk. "I'll

come with you. Not because I want to, and not because you challenged me. But because I want to show you exactly how ridiculous you are." He hesitated. Then he added, "So where is Sergei?"

"Where else would Sergei be?" Genshiro asked, half laughing. "He's getting the girls."

Chapter Seven

It was only a few yards from Karl's window to the corner, where an ornamental trellis covered a very structural iron pipe. Alice was tying the rope to one of the cross braces, pulling in short, practiced jerks.

"That'll hold now," she announced after checking it yet again. "Can't believe that none of you ever tied a knot except for your scouting rank."

"Pioneers," Sergei mumbled. "And I didn't do camping. I did space and astronomy and chess."

"And a fat lot of good it did you when it comes to tying rope," Alice retorted briskly.

"Shut up and let's go," Lanie said. She took the rope in her hands to steady herself and climbed down the struts on the pipe with ease. Sergei shrugged and followed when Lanie reached the ground. He wasn't about to be shown up twice in ten minutes. When he released the rope, Nathan went without incident, as did Alice after him.

Noemi looked down and then cast a pleading look at Genshiro. "Could I please please use the stairs?" she begged. "I've never climbed a drainpipe before, and my clothes . . ."

Her leather miniskirt and spike-heeled shoes were not made for climbing.

"Don't be such a baby, Noemi," Alice whispered loudly. "Throw me down your shoes and you can get on your sneakers like I told you to in the first place."

Noemi whimpered and looked fragile. Alice shook her head. Lanie turned her back. Gen touched her shoulder. "Look, if you're scared, I'll hold on to you while you change your shoes," he whispered in her ear. "No one ever has to know."

She managed a small smile and sat on the wide ledge. She dropped the shoes onto the grass, where they landed without a sound. Then she grabbed the rope, felt for a foothold, and slipped.

Gen, already seated and ready to climb down, shot out a hand and caught her. "Steady," he told her. "Small movements."

"I told you this was a stupid idea," Karl said triumphantly.

"If you say that one more time, Karl, you can go down without the benefit of the rope or the drainpipe," Gen countered. Then, as Noemi stumbled onto the thick grass, he went over the side hand over hand and was down in a flash.

Karl, left alone on the ledge, took a moment to consider. The others were staring at him, waiting. He felt forced, angry, but there was nothing else to do except climb down and join them.

All together, the seven team members walked across the large lawn to the perimeter of the complex.

"What are we going to do about a car?" Karl demanded. "How are we going to get into town? You don't mean we're going to steal one? I won't. I'll report you—"

Noemi giggled and cut him off. "We don't need to steal a car," she said. She dug in her purse, didn't watch her footing, and caught a heel in the soft ground. She fell in a heap, making a little sobbing sound.

"Are you okay?" Sergei asked.

Noemi nodded bravely and then sat comfortably to inspect the damage. It was minimal. Her skirt had a few streaks of mud, but a damp towel would clean that up. And her shoes looked terrible. But she wasn't hurt at all, and she stood gingerly, not certain that she trusted the grass.

"Can we walk on the path?" she asked plaintively.

They moved over the six or seven meters to the white pavement without comment. "I told you those were stupid shoes," Alice hissed. "Why didn't you keep on your sneakers?"

Noemi shrugged in answer. Then she returned her attention to her purse. After a little more digging she drew out a set of keys. "Daddy loaned me the Mercedes while I'm here," she said, smiling at Karl. "If you want, you can drive."

Sergei navigated and Karl drove. Cruising the Houston highways, Karl slipped the car through the traffic like a phantom in the night. He was good. Better than good, and a small smile tugged at his mouth. They were doing an even fifty-five, straight on the limit, when one of the huge Suburbans favored by Houstonians barreled into the center lane, obviously blind to their presence.

Karl eased them out into the left. Sergei winced as the oversize bumper of the Suburban swerved within inches of the Mercedes, but Karl was in perfect control. They were never touched.

"Hey, you're great at that, man, you really are," Gen said.

Karl smiled. "This is a great car. I could drive all night."

"Well, please don't," Alice called from the backseat. "I'm starving."

Sergei looked at the map once more and realized that they had passed the exit. Surprisingly, Karl didn't get angry. They had to get off the highway, turn around, and try again before they located the major street and the turquoise T-bird mounted on a high pylon over the cafe.

The Hard Rock Cafe was famous for its loud music and its clientele, both of which were going full blast when the group arrived. The noise from the music videos on the TV made it impossible to talk, but Nathan didn't really care. He was too busy trying to catch the vids and the people. There were a couple of real glamsters in tiger-striped spandex pants and bleached-blond hair teased and moussed within an inch of the ceiling.

"Are they famous?" Alice asked, her eyes wide.

As Nathan looked at Alice, he suddenly realized she looked different. And pretty. He had never thought of hardworking, pale Alice as pretty but in that off-the-shoulder blouse with her jeans, and her hair loose and rippling, she was transformed.

"Not famous," Nathan said, trying to be offhand. "Probably just with a local band."

Gen was inspecting the collection of guitars along the wall while Noemi was turning heads. Sergei had gone to the bar and was talking to the bartender, a young woman with very long legs in a very short skirt. Nathan couldn't help comparing the bartender's legs to Noemi's and decided Noemi's were just as good. Lanie looked as much like a professional rocker as the glam boys Alice had pointed out. In her torn jeans with the handcuff belt, black bustier, and heavy black earrings against her bright yellow hair, she could almost pass for Lita Ford. They were all his team, and they were hot. Even Karl seemed relaxed for once. He had gone with Sergei to get the drinks.

And the music was great. "You want to dance?" Alice asked. Nathan didn't need to be asked twice.

When they got back to the table, Karl and Gen were in a heated discussion. "No, we don't need the extra power," Karl was saying. "It needs to be lightweight and easy to conceal. Remember, we have only what we can carry with us."

"Yeah, but it won't take much more and we'll get a lot more range. And fuel. You didn't mention fuel," Gen replied.

"Do it on batteries," Alice spoke up. "No guarantee that anyplace'll be nearby, or open."

The vehicle. Whatever it was they were creating for the survival trek, this was the first time they were really getting it together. Karl knew more about engines, about vehicles, than all the rest of them. Nathan got caught up in the excitement, keyed up by the strong beat of the music and the flashing videos.

"I think the navigation's going to be the big thing," Lanie said softly. "If we program in the sun's position and all the local maps, that should be some help."

"Can you do it?" Karl asked, excited.

Lanie smiled. "No problem. But I'll trade you for another coke. This stuff hits the spot."

"And we'd better enjoy it now, because there won't be any more when we get to Mars," Alice moaned.

Gen shook his head. "No, that is not a difficult problem. The recipe is a secret but we'll analyze a sample of it in the chem lab and then once we get to Mars, we can sell our output for major money."

"That's capitalist," Sergei said, shocked.

"Absolutely!" Gen agreed.

"There isn't going to be any money on Mars," Alice said. "Probably we'll trade for things."

"Okay, who'll trade water and atmosphere for a year's supply of coke?" Gen asked very loudly.

The whole group laughed so hard that they were all gasping for breath. Nathan's sides hurt.

"Yeah," he said when he had stopped shaking. "Remember all those stupid old sci-fi movies? You know the ones where there are all these aliens on Mars and they want to take over the Earth?"

"That's just because of the canals," Karl protested, joining in the fun. "When they didn't know that they were just crevasses."

"I saw that movie. Two itty-bitty polar caps and the movie people make it out that half the planet is Antarctica. Mars needs women!" Lanie chimed in.

"No!" Sergei protested in horror. "If Mars doesn't have women, I'm not going!"

And Nathan forgot what he was going to say as they all laughed again.

Just then the food came, and it was good. Of course,

84

compared to what they'd been eating at the space center, TV dinners would have tasted good. But the burgers were charbroiled and the fries crisp and hot, and Nathan relished every bite. He was so wrapped up in the food that at first he didn't notice Gen gesturing urgently toward the front door. Sergei had gone dead white and Alice was biting her nails. What was going on? It wasn't until Lanie tapped him on the forearm and pointed his head in the right direction that Nathan saw.

A very tall black man dressed in an Italian-style suit with a very pretty woman were all he saw. So what? Then the man turned to talk to the woman. The man was Dr. Thompson.

Nathan hunched down, trying to make himself as small as possible. He couldn't take his eyes off the supervisor. Like a mouse hypnotized by a snake, he couldn't look away. And then Dr. Thompson raised his eyes and saw them. It was all over.

Around the table seven hopeful space explorers cringed. Only Noemi seemed oblivious to their predicament. "I like his suit!" she said approvingly, craning her neck for a better view. "And is that his girlfriend? I wonder if she's coming too, or if maybe he's telling her good-bye. Or maybe she's telling him that she won't go with him because she can't leave home. It's so romantic."

"Well, no matter what he's telling her, he's going to be telling us that we're not going anywhere at all. Except maybe home," Alice said. She looked miserable.

The worst was about to happen. Dr. Thompson was heading directly for their table. No hope remained. Only prayer.

Towering over them, Dr. Lawrence Thompson looked like a few megatons about to explode. "What are you doing here?" His voice carried over the loud music as if it were merely soft background. "In case you idiots didn't realize it, some of those rules are meant for your safety. We hand-pick you for the greatest adventure in the human race, and all you can think about is running around for rock music and soda. You don't even deserve your airfare home as far as I'm concerned."

A stunned silence followed. It was Karl, neatly dressed in pressed slacks and his hair combed back, who answered in a measured voice. "Excuse me, sir, but if the food and the entertainment at the center were a little better, we wouldn't be tempted to break all the rules and leave the area. As it is, I know my father would find it quite normal for me to go out to eat and listen to music and drink sodas with my friends. And we have the use of Noemi's car and we don't have class tomorrow until ten in the morning. Every one of us has had a parent's permission to have some social life. We are not doing anything illegal, dangerous, or immoral. I suggest that the rules are unreasonable, not our behavior."

"Yeah," Lanie added. "And you don't have to eat that glop they call food every night, and there's no MTV. We're not dead, you know."

Dr. Thompson glowered at them. "You're right, you're not dead. You're just going to wish you were. I suggest that you get in that car and get back to the center immediately. By which I mean this second or sooner. Believe me, the entire selection committee is going to hear about this."

There was nothing else to do. They paid the bill.

Nathan left half his burger on his plate, but he wasn't hungry anymore anyway. He rose and left as Dr. Thompson watched them. The rest of the team followed him back to the parking lot to the silver-gray Mercedes with foreign plates. They got in silently, each taking the place they had taken on the trip out. That seemed about a million years before.

"You were great, Karl," Nathan said. "It took real guts to stand up to Thompson like that."

Karl turned the key in the ignition, and then turned the car off. "I want you to understand one thing, Nathan," he said very softly. "You are responsible for all of us failing. This stupid, juvenile idea of yours just got all of us kicked out of the program."

Nathan felt a lead ball in the middle of his stomach. He wanted to be sick. He had really done it this time. Karl was right. Everything was gone and it was all his fault. All on a prank, a stupid little game to get around the rules and have a little fun.

They were halfway back to the center when Lanie spoke up. "You know, you're all a bunch of wusses. I kicked butt to get into this program, and I'm not just gonna roll over and play dead. That's just what they want. Thompson, Suki Long—all those creeps. You gonna play their game? You a bunch of quitters? I'll bet real money that that's what it's all about. They want to find out if you've got the guts it takes to survive when it's all going against you, because I'll bet it's gonna be that way on Mars a whole lot. Are you going to make it, or are you just going to give up? You can say a lot about me, but no one ever said I was a coward—or a quitter."

Something in what Lanie said made sense. "Okay,"

Nathan said, hesitating. "You can count me in."

"And me," Gen chimed in.

They drove the rest of the way in stony silence, but this time it was the silence of resolve.

Chapter Eight

"We are very fortunate here in Houston to be able to visit the lab at the University of Houston that is perhaps the foremost in the world in the field of superconductors. We will be at that facility next Monday, and those of you who choose to specialize in this area will apprentice there. We have been given permission to place four interns." Dr. Thompson surveyed the group, and Nathan wished he could crawl under his seat.

"Naturally the work you'd do as an intern isn't the most exciting, but you would learn to make the ceramic mixes that are our most promising superconductors right now."

"But if this technology isn't generally available, how will we make it work in an alien environment?" someone asked.

"You mean, if we can't use it, how come we have to study it," Nathan muttered under his breath. Dr. Thompson was already at the board, though, and didn't hear him. As if that could make things worse.

"Well, David, we have a lot more than theory. And we'll need all the energy we can get once we arrive on

Mars. Remember, there never were any dinosaurs or prehistoric plant life to create oil or coal there. And the other major source of energy here on Earth is hydro-electric. But Mars doesn't have oceans or rivers. In short, our energy supplies will be quite limited. With this new technology we'll have the energy and we'll be able to keep our new world unpolluted. Which will also be very important while we reinforce and oxygenize the Martian atmosphere.

"As you all know, electricity is usually channeled through wires or some other form of metal. When that happens, the molecules in the metal get in the way of the electrons traveling through it, and the electrons lose energy. In fact, nearly half the electricity generated in a city like Houston is eaten up just getting into people's homes, before you even turn on a light. This is not very efficient, but at the moment is the only way we can make it work. And I guess we all think it's worth it to have our blow dryers and telephones. But think of how you would feel if you had to walk through water up to your waist to get wherever you were going. That would tire you out very quickly.

"But with superconductivity, the waste is almost eliminated. And we all know that waste not, want not is an explorer's creed. Some materials, chilled down to just about absolute zero, react differently with the electrons. No one knows just why — there's a lot about electricity we don't know — but the electrons align and move in pairs. For some reason this eliminates most of the resistance, and they move as easily as you or I do through air. But can you identify the problem with this?"

"It is quite difficult to create temperatures near absolute zero," Suki Long said, obviously quite pleased with herself, "which is minus 273.15 degrees Celsius or minus 459.67 degrees Fahrenheit."

"Show off!" Sergei muttered to Gen, who was sitting next to him.

"That's true, Suki," Dr. Thompson said. "But recently at the University of Houston, Dr. Paul Chu developed a ceramic material that doesn't need to be nearly that cold. And so there may be some very solid applications to our own work. Anyway, we'll be there next Monday, so get ready to be creative."

"Sounds like great stuff—for the dark side of Mercury," Gen muttered.

Class was over and it was time for lunch, and Dr. Thompson still hadn't said anything further about the previous night. Nathan couldn't stand the torture anymore. His father had always told him to confront trouble head-on. So he lingered while the others filed out of the room.

It took a few seconds for the supervisor to realize that he wasn't alone. He glanced up and seemed surprised to see Nathan still in his seat. He looked mildly curious and interested, and absolutely benign. "Did you want to discuss something?" he asked reasonably.

Nathan sighed and forced himself to sit up. "About last night. When are we going to hear?" he asked heavily.

Dr. Thompson seemed confused. "Hear what about last night?"

"Are we getting kicked out, or put on probation or something?"

It took a moment for the supervisor to connect. And then he shook his head. "Probation? You didn't do any-

91

thing exactly illegal, did you? Didn't borrow a car without permission?"

Nathan shook his head.

"Let's just say you've been lucky this time," Dr. Thompson said evenly. "We require a certain amount of discipline in the people we choose, and we're not happy with your behavior. But there remains the fact that your team has extremely high ratings in math, computers, geology, and physics. To say nothing of excellent physical recommendations. So there will be no official action taken. But believe me, one more stunt like that and you'll all be out on the street."

"Huh?" Nathan asked. He wasn't sure he was hearing right. They were off the hook this time? Lanie had been right. Next they'd have him believing that frogs could fly.

"Why don't you go eat lunch?" Dr. Thompson asked. "And stop looking like you're going to get your head cut off. We've got a full afternoon ahead."

Dr. Thompson was not kidding. They were scheduled for two hours of physical conditioning. "I feel like I'm in the army," Sergei groused as they changed into shorts and T-shirts. "Why can't we just play sports?"

They met the girls out on the field. Lanie had put on a cut-up White Lion T-shirt with her gym shorts and Noemi was sporting a new pair of Reeboks that matched her bright red nail polish. Alice had her braids pinned up on her head. "Come on," Alice was saying. "Let's get warmed up."

"I don't want to waste any energy until we really have to begin," Noemi complained. "I hate this. What does this have to do with science anyway? What's it got to do with Mars?"

"It's gonna get us there," Lanie interrupted. "So I don't care if they're asking us to sing 'Mary Had a Little Lamb.' You got it?"

Noemi nodded miserably just as the instructor called them all together on the field. It was obstacle-course day. "Good all-around workout and working on skills that might be important. Running, climbing. Okay, teams together and we'll start."

"Why do we have to worry about climbing when the gravity's going to be different anyway?" Noemi sniffed.

Karl made a face. "Look, Noemi, there isn't any way out except to do it."

And they did do it. Over and over and over until they all ached and dropped on the grass. Noemi looked about ready to cry.

"But you did great," Nathan said. "You got through the whole course twice, just like everyone else. You're getting better."

His muscles ached so much that all Nathan wanted to do was lie down. He'd gone full out on the course, knowing that the team needed every point they could muster. His arms and legs were trembling with exhaustion, and all he wanted to do was go to sleep. A quick shower and a long night in bed, that was what he wanted. A mattress never felt so good.

The knock at the door was crisp and precise. Nathan couldn't figure out who it was. Sergei had the key and Gen would try the door first. And it was open. Nathan didn't have any reason to lock up anything, let alone himself. So when he told the caller to come in, he was expecting something different.

What he wasn't expecting was Karl, and Karl as grim-faced and angry as Karl could be. And that was not a pleasant sight at all. He was holding out a manila envelope as if it could accuse Nathan in person.

"What's up, Karl?" Nathan asked.

Karl didn't say anything. Instead, he dumped the contents of the envelope on the floor at Nathan's feet. For some reason that bothered Nathan more than anything Karl had done before. "Cut the cheap melodrama," he said harshly. "Just tell me what's going on."

Karl smiled unpleasantly and pointed to the pile. "You won't believe me if I said anything. There's the proof."

"Of what?" Nathan was practically screaming now. He hated being interrupted, and, even more, he hated Karl's attitude. Here in his own room too. That made it even worse.

Still, he glanced at what had fallen out of the envelope. Nothing much, really. A learner's permit, a school ID card, a couple of letters with a school letterhead. Nothing very interesting.

"Look at the names," Karl said.

Nathan shook his head but picked up the school ID, curious. The picture was clearly Lanie. But the name was Johnson, not Rizzo. The same was true of the learner's permit. Nathan had a feeling he didn't want to look at the school letters.

"How did you get this stuff?" he asked.

Karl shrugged. "Not your business. But I think the other thing is. The fact that she's here under a false name. Maybe she wasn't the person who really was accepted. Maybe she isn't even capable of keeping up with us. Maybe she's here to spy. But this isn't just a night out in a restaurant. This is serious."

Nathan swallowed hard. It was serious, all right. But to his mind, how Karl had gotten hold of the documents was even more serious. "You'd go and narc on your own teammate?" he asked, not believing that anyone had that little honor. "Who else knows?"

Karl turned away. "You mean, if you can shut me up, who else do you have to track down? Because somebody is going to blow the whistle on this one. Nobody is going to cover up for a liar and a sneak."

Nathan's mind was racing. There were a million possible answers. Maybe she had changed her name, like she'd been adopted by a stepfather. Happened all the time. Or she'd discovered who her real father was and decided to use his name. That was something he could understand, and he told Karl that very clearly.

"Then look at the letters."

Nathan looked and his stomach contorted. It was a letter from an educational testing service to a school, saying that a girl by the name of Cindy Rizzo was reasonably able to handle any normal assignment, but that she showed no special aptitude or interest in space science, and should therefore not be considered a candidate for the To Mars Together program. The second letter was a memo to the school board that computer security had been breached again and that, according to several teachers' classroom books, grades had been changed. And it speculated that the only student in the school who could have pulled it off was named Lanie Johnson.

The third one was a school record for one Lanie

Rizzo, complete with social security number and teachers' comments. That seemed straightforward enough, until he turned the page. There, on a green and white lined printout, were records for both Lanie Johnson and Cindy Rizzo. And how the two had been meshed to create Lanie's current identity.

"But why?" Nathan asked himself.

"Ask her," Karl sneered. "I guess because she wasn't good enough to get in on her own."

"But if she could pull this stuff on secured computers, then she'd have to be good enough," Nathan said in near awe. He'd tried once to change a grade in the school computer, and not only got kicked out of the system, but traced as well. He'd been on Saturday detention for a month for that.

"I think we'd better have a team meeting before we do anything," he said softly.

Karl glared. "What we have to do is obvious. If we don't, we're as guilty as she is."

Nathan looked up, his face set firm. "We're in the United States, and someone is innocent until proven guilty."

"I think this is proof enough," Karl said.

"You might not like the rest of us, Karl, but you have to admit that we're in this together. We should talk to Lanie. Everyone on the team should know. I'll call the girls. Gen's in the basement practice room. If you can get him and round up Sergei, we'll meet out by the fountain in half an hour. Okay?"

Karl gave a half-superior smile and left. Nathan felt as if he were looking over the edge of a cliff. His stomach swayed and his palms were sweaty. Roger from another team was on the dorm phone when Nathan got to the end of the hall. He growled and told Roger he'd be only a minute and that it was an emergency. The other guy shook his head, shrugged, and hung up.

He was relieved that when he got through it was Alice who came to the phone. Nathan didn't want to talk to Lanie yet, didn't know how to talk to her or what to say. Alice, however, accepted his terse explanation that there was a team emergency and could she round up the girls and get them over to the fountain. Relieved, Nathan headed over himself. He wanted to be there early, to be out of the oppressive walls of the dorm, to think.

He had barely been in Houston for a month and already it seemed to be his whole life. Everything from before had taken on the quality of the pictures in his mother's photo album. Not that the past was forgotten, merely that he had changed so much that it felt as if it had happened to another person.

Back home he never would have had to deal with problems like these. And his future, his real future, was never on the line every day. Because at home, if you messed up, you were still a kid and could maybe have a second chance. Nothing was final. And you had some idea of how people would act. Not like Karl turning Lanie in. Nathan still didn't understand that one.

In the early evening light the fountain sparkled. The main campus of the space center was magical at this hour, when there were no tourists around. Nathan hadn't thought about why he had chosen this place to meet, and only now that he was there and surrounded by the low buildings did he realize that he found it both comforting and inspiring. They were in the center of the real space effort here. Not just dreams and futures,

97

but the daily work of keeping NASA flying.

He saw them coming up the walk, dark shadows in the friendly glow of the path lights. All together, it seemed, although he couldn't tell in the dark. He felt vaguely ill and wished it were all a bad dream that would go away. More than that, he hated Karl. He hated the other boy's gloating expression as he destroyed their group. He hated how Karl had made everything so difficult, didn't care about how anyone else felt and what everyone else wanted. Karl was out to ground them all, and suddenly Nathan's anger turned colder and more to the attitude of justice. For some reason of his own, Karl was out to get all of them. Nathan saw that clearly in a single flash, although he couldn't understand it. If Karl got all of them, he would get himself too. Why did Karl want to destroy himself?

Nathan saw the pattern clearly, all woven together as a single thing. And just as he realized that it wasn't the rest of the team that Karl hated, but himself, they all arrived. He had to pull himself back to reality. But now he knew how he was going to handle the crisis.

Chapter Nine

"An emergency?" Alice said hollowly, looking around in the shadows. "What kind of emergency could we have?"

Nathan sat down on the edge of the fountain. He explained the problem and handed over the ID and letters that Karl had given him as evidence. "But I think we have to give Lanie the benefit of the doubt. She should at least have a chance to explain before we do anything."

Lanie got up and looked at them all warily. Her bleached-blond hair fell across her face, and in the dark her skin looked as white as the concrete all framed in shadow. She turned and pushed her hands deeper into the pockets of her leather jacket. She huddled under the leather as if it would protect her. Then she turned around and glared back at her team, her eyes flashing with defiance.

"Explain? Yeah, right, explain," Lanie said, her voice thick with anger. "None of you even knows what tough means. Nobody's tough because they want to be. Just that you don't dare let them see what's inside, that you're a person and you care and you bleed when you're cut just like anybody else. You don't know what it's like living in the projects, in the wrong part of town. Where no matter what you do you're wrong, you're no good, you're nothing but a liar and a cheat and a cheap piece of flesh to use and burn up and spit out.

"They keep saying that you can make it if you have the ability. That's a fairy tale, I mean like 'Cinderella' or something. Only in real life there isn't any fairy godmother. There's only the rent and the welfare people who talk about getting good jobs. Only the kind of jobs they're talking about are word processing or computer operator. No college or graduate school, no systems engineer for Lanie Johnson. No, my dreams are just supposed to be a steady paycheck and a husband who doesn't beat me."

Lanie tossed her head, curled her lip, and looked defiant. "I haven't done badly," she said proudly. "Have I? I haven't done worse than anyone else on any of the projects, right? And I can outprogram any of you. Any of those other bozos too. And you all know it. Nobody can make a system run the way I can, and you can't deny it.

"Yeah, I changed my name. So what? There isn't any law against it. I want to go more than any six of you put together. I'm not going to hold us back. You want to see where the problem is, look at Karl and how he's running all over the place making trouble for us."

"I'm not making trouble," Karl protested. "I'm the only one who even tries to obey the rules and keep us from getting tossed out of here. And if anything is going to get us into trouble, it's this."

100

Lanie looked at them hard. "It isn't going to get out," she said firmly.

"It already has," Nathan pointed out.

Lanie looked at her feet. "I guess it was really stupid to keep that stuff. I don't even know why I did. To remind myself, I guess."

Nathan thought he'd never seen a girl look so mean. Lanie's eyes glittered hard in the starlight, and her face was tilted in disdain more convincing than he'd ever seen in any girls in school. So he was more than a little startled when Noemi went over to Lanie and put her arm around the street girl.

"Really, Lanie, it doesn't matter. I don't care. Tomorrow we'll go shopping and buy something nice and forget about this," Noemi said in a soothing voice.

Then Lanie broke. Her legs seemed to buckle under her and she collapsed to sit on the grass. Her face twisted and the glitter became tears running down her face.

"You don't know what it's like," she sobbed. Noemi took out a delicate lace-edged handkerchief and silently handed it to Lanie.

Lanie seemed to take strength from that gesture. She took a deep breath and twisted the hankie in her hands. "You don't know what it's like," she started again slowly. "Whenever things were really bad at home, I used to think about how I was going to build an artificial intelligence computer all my own, and have an office in the university and be able to spend all my time doing what I liked best. Since there weren't any computers in school for me to work on, I learned how to work on the one for school records. I taught myself, pretty much.

101

During office detention. I was supposed to be in the office then.

"And then I tried to join the Math Club at school, and the chess team. And I was pretty good, until Mrs. Barrett looked up my records and saw how many detentions I'd gotten and said that I couldn't be in the clubs until my record was better. And that those clubs were for kids who were going somewhere and that I wasn't one of them. That I was a no-good lazy little loser, that's what she called me.

"And then I found out about the To Mars Together program and I knew, I knew I belonged. For the very first time there was a place where I had to be, where it didn't matter where I came from or what my mother did or how poor she was. All that mattered was that I was smart, and I could prove it.

"And I did. I used Cindy's last name and her address and changed my own records. But I had to take all the same tests the rest of you did, and score as well." She looked up defiantly through her tears.

"I don't think there's anything that the authorities need to know," Alice said quite crisply.

Nathan agreed silently. He couldn't help but think that not very much separated him from Lanie. His mother had had a good job, that was all. And he'd been encouraged at school.

"It's agreed, then," Nathan said carefully. "We don't tell anyone. We'll have to destroy this stuff. Lanie, you want to take care of that?"

Lanie blew her nose and shook her head.

"I'll do it," Noemi said brightly. "We'll go to the beach on Sunday and I'll throw them out to sea. That's very romantic. It belongs on TV."

Everyone laughed at that. Even Lanie couldn't resist joining in. Then the laughing led to a silly craziness that swept them all up. Sergei jumped in the fountain and began splashing the others with water. Gen and Nathan jumped in after him and wrestled him until they got his head underwater, at which point Alice gave Gen a good shove and the three boys flopped together.

When they got out of the water, Sergei chased Alice and tackled her on the grass. The game quickly became a cross between tag and splashing as they grew rowdier.

Only when they were out of energy and flopped down together on the grass did Nathan notice that Karl was gone.

Dripping wet, the six of them staggered back to the dorm just before the doors were locked. The lobby and stairwells bore wet tracks to their rooms. But Nathan hardly felt the chill as he wondered what happened to Karl.

"He just didn't want to play," Sergei insisted. "He wouldn't go against all of us like that. He couldn't."

Dried off and dressed again, Nathan went down to the TV room. He couldn't concentrate enough to study and he couldn't sleep. As he sat in front of the glowing picture with the sound turned off, he heard something from what seemed to be very far away. It was music, but not the kind of music he and Gen had on tape.

It was from a piano, very lush and romantic. It made Nathan think of the movies his mother liked, those British films where people talked a lot in cars and were a little strange. He didn't recognize it at all, but that didn't matter. He hadn't ever been too interested in classical music.

He followed the sound through a door on the far side of the TV room. There, tucked away where he had never noticed it before, was a tiny room with a large piano. At the piano sat Karl Muller, concentrating so hard on the music that he didn't notice Nathan's arrival.

Nathan stood and said nothing. He let the music flow over him and, even if it wasn't the kind of music he generally liked, he could understand the hurt and anger in the playing. He listened. Karl was very good, surprisingly good. And then the piece ended and Karl looked up and breathed as if he were coming up from under deep water.

Only after a few breaths did Karl notice Nathan standing in the doorway. "What do you want?" he asked coldly.

"You play very well," Nathan said carefully. "I'd have thought that you and Gen'd have a lot more in common, with the music. Why didn't you try out for the center orchestra?"

Karl turned away. "It's none of your business," he said.

"Sort of like Lanie," Nathan said slowly.

"No. Nothing like Lanie," Karl retorted.

"Did you turn her in?" Nathan said.

"You all agreed not to," Karl replied. "You agreed. No one asked me. But if you really want an answer, no. Not yet, anyway."

Karl looked down at the keyboard and began to play

104

something that Nathan was certain that he had never heard before.

Nathan was tired and torn and angry and sad all at once. It shouldn't be up to him to make this all work. They should all be making it work together, and there should be someone to help. He shouldn't have to do it alone.

Part III:
November

Chapter Ten

Their team was the first scheduled for the tank. After ages of classroom work they were finally going to get a taste of space and they were all excited.

The tank was just an oversize swimming pool, but what went on in it would give Flipper nightmares. Conditions underwater were the closest anyone could come to simulating weightlessness on Earth. In a full space suit, astronauts practiced various tasks with the aid of divers. Just moving in a zero-gravity environment was disorienting, and in order to actually accomplish any work in space it was necessary to practice.

This was their first chance at a practical space exercise, and they were all excited. "Nothing fancy this time around," Dr. Thompson said. "Just get the feeling of zero G and no local vertical. That's going to be real important when we're out. Dr. Matinez will take you through the paces. Good luck." He waved and left to join another team at some other training activity.

Alice, Gen, and Sergei were arguing over who got to go first. "Not that it's important, since we're all getting a turn," Sergei said, leaving the field.

Gen pulled out a quarter. "Call it in the air," he said, and Alice immediately asked for heads. She won the toss and began to suit up. The suiting process took so long that the other six of them worked out an order so they wouldn't waste any tank time. To make life a little easier, there was a minicrane to help get the thing on.

First came climbing down into the bottom half, and then the top was hoisted overhead and lowered. The hard part was scrunching in through the metal rings at the middle, the neck, and the arms. That and the weight. Space suits were not made to be comfortable. The helmet wasn't bad, but the gloves were so bulky that it was hard to move fingers. All the fine control was gone. It reminded Alice of wearing ski gloves.

Once completely sealed inside the suit, Alice was lowered into the tank. The suit had been specially modified so that a breathing tube ran to the surface, and there were two divers on duty to move either the astronaut or the equipment in response to mechanical devices on command. They were also there to make sure the air tube was always clear.

Nathan watched for a while in fascination. He especially liked the way the divers moved, and how Alice seemed to get upside down so easily. He knew that no local vertical meant that in zero G there wasn't anything that felt like "up" but he couldn't really appreciate it.

Until it was his turn to go down.

The sensation was—dreamlike. Immersed in the tank, he was drifting, comfortable in a way he had never been before. And the space! The tank had looked smallish from the outside, and he knew that if he had his normal senses, it wouldn't be much larger. But without any feeling at all that one way was "up" and another "down," all the possible places opened up the space so that everyplace was useful. Suddenly he understood that on a spaceship the ceiling really was the same as the floor or the walls, and that gave them four times as much usable space.

Nathan felt great relief. He hadn't realized how much the small, cramped quarters of the shuttle had bothered him until he realized that in zero G there would be much more usable room. That, and the fact that he suddenly understood why furniture wasn't necessary. Sitting was no more comfortable than floating in any other position. Only the drifting got to him.

Every time he moved an arm or leg, his whole body swung slowly in the opposite direction. "Try to reach the shuttle mock-up," a voice came in his helmet. The mock-up wasn't far, but somehow he seemed to get all twisted around trying to approach it. And no matter how much energy he felt, everything was very slow, as if the tank were filled not with water but with half-firm Jell-O.

All right. There had to be a way to do this. He positioned himself so that he was headed toward the mock door like an arrow. He raised his arms very very slowly, trying to negate as much of the back-push as he could. Then he swooped down with some force, which propelled him forward.

It worked. Not the most elegant solution, certainly, but it worked. He was sure there was some other, approved method of getting around that didn't make a person look like a giant turtle. But it was better than drifting aimlessly.

"Very good," the voice congratulated him. "Time to

109

come up."

The divers attached him to the hoist, and he was pulled from the water. Getting out of the suit was almost as uncomfortable as getting in, and took nearly as long.

When they had all had their turns and were dressed in street clothes again, they were all conducted to a conference room. One of the smallest side perks of the program, Nathan thought. They got to use these luxurious quarters for classrooms, with their upholstered chairs and unmarked tables. It was a million times nicer than Washington-Fairfield High.

Glancing around at his teammates, he could see the excitement on all their faces. Even Karl was shining a little around the edges. And Lanie was glowing as if she were radioactive.

"You know," she was saying, "what if instead of going to Mars we built a high orbital shell and lived without gravity forever?"

"Then we couldn't ever come back," Sergei said sadly. "The cosmonauts in *Salyut* had a lot of trouble readjusting to gravity after only a few months in orbit. They couldn't even walk when they landed. They had to be taken out in wheelchairs."

"Exactly," a stranger said, entering the room. She was tiny, smaller than Noemi, and wore huge glasses that seemed too heavy for her face. There was something crisp in her manner and her expression. "Do you know what the problem is?"

They all thought for a moment. "Exercise?" Sergei ventured. "If you don't have to use your muscles, they get weak."

The woman nodded. "That's the first reason. And

that's why you'll all be required to take an hour of exercise a day as long as you're in transit. But there's something else. Any guesses?"

They all looked blankly at one another. Nathan didn't realize that a long period in space could cause muscular weakness, let alone anything else.

The woman smiled. "I just hope you all like to drink lots of milk and eat ice cream."

"Yuch," Gen said, his face screwing up. "I hate that stuff."

"Well, there's always broccoli," she answered. "You see, in a zero G environment, calcium passes out of the bones in large quantities. This depletion leads to pressure fractures as soon as a person is reintroduced to gravity. The only way we know to counter this is plenty of exercise and calcium supplements. But it's better to get nutrients from food, as opposed to pills."

"But what are we going to do on Mars?" Alice asked. "We won't have the capacity for dairy farming for a long time."

The woman nodded gravely. "Indeed. We are currently looking for additional sources that will be practical in that situation. There are the vegetables, like broccoli, and small fish bones. I know you'll be bringing fish eggs to hatch."

"Wait a minute. What's wrong with cows?" Lanie demanded. "And how do you know we can't bring 'em?"

Alice began to laugh hard. "Because I grew up on a farm, that's how I know. Cows are very big and they eat a lot. Which seems obvious, I suppose, but you can't very well put them in a transport craft. And all the fodder they would need on the trip, not to mention once we had the fields going and surplus for them to eat."

Lanie looked at Alice as if she were crazy. Even Gen and Karl seemed a little shocked. Sergei nodded vigorously. "I worked on a farm for one month in the summer," he said excitedly. "And the cows did nothing but eat all day. We had more grain for the cows than for all the other animals combined. Including the people."

They all laughed. Even Karl had to smile.

"Speaking of eating . . ." Nathan reminded them.

The woman smiled and nodded. "Almost time for dinner," she agreed. "But I would like you all to think about one more factor. In addition to calcium loss, we still don't understand what living on another planet will do to your natural rhythms. Over the long run, that is. A Mars day is only slightly longer than Earth's, twenty-four hours and thirty-seven minutes, which makes it a good candidate for a colony. But even those few minutes could create a certain imbalance. The Department of Space Medicine is going to be monitoring you very closely during the entire run of the project."

"You mean for the rest of our lives," Gen muttered.

"Yes," the teacher agreed without any hesitation. "And we hope that you will eventually be glad that we did. Now, how about some dinner?"

The workout in the tank must have taken more energy than Nathan had thought. He was famished, and ate two large helpings of everything. Even if it was just the usual rotten cafeteria food.

But he wasn't so hungry that he didn't notice Karl sitting with Suki Long and her teammates. Karl had done that every night this week, and Nathan couldn't figure out why. Sure, Karl had always thought Suki had a better team and a better chance of going to Mars.

112

Only there was something that struck him as a little suspicious. Sergei's constant reminder that Karl was probably just a little in love with Suki didn't carry weight with Nathan. Sergei thought like that about all the girls, except for the ones on his team, who were like sisters. And it didn't feel right to Nathan. Karl didn't look at Suki as if he liked her. More as if he were trying to impress her.

He must have stared at them for a long time, because Alice caught his eye and shook her head slowly. "Don't worry," she said under her breath. "When the ratings come out, he'll see how good we are."

Gen raised an eyebrow in question. "And how do you know we're good?" he asked.

"Noemi's been keeping score," Alice answered. "And we've got to be in the top quarter."

"Unless our demerits have messed us up. We're not the only ones around here who are any good," Lanie said flatly. "Remember, they said that everyone here's qualified."

Nathan knew exactly what she meant. All his life he had always been the best. He'd never had to work at it. It just was, a fact that went along with his sandy brown hair or his right-handedness. Until he'd come to Houston. All of a sudden he wasn't nearly the best anymore. All these other kids were as good as he was. Every one of them could do anything he could, except maybe some really radical air on a skateboard.

Part of him was overjoyed that he could finally talk to people who understood the way he thought, and still weren't geeks. Well, at least most of them weren't geeks. A few exceptions didn't matter.

Another part of him felt afraid and cheated. Being

the best had always been so easy before. Now, for the very first time in his life, there was competition. He had to work really hard just to keep up, when before he hardly had to work at all to show up the teachers.

The competition was frightening. He had never even considered the possibility of losing before. Not that he really did now. He couldn't believe that his team wouldn't be selected. That just was not real. Could not be real. But the other candidates were good. Some, he was truly afraid, might even be better than he was. And that made him jealous for the very first time in his life.

For a moment he panicked at the thought of the teams being publicly ranked. What if he wasn't on the top the way he always had been before?

But he wasn't the only one who felt that way. He was just too shy to admit it. Gen said the words for all of them. "When I was in school, regular school, I didn't have to do anything. Just show up once in a while, and there I was on the top. You know, this is the only time in my life I've ever had to work at anything. But what's really strange is, I sort of like it."

Nathan laughed along with the rest of them but kept his feelings to himself.

Chapter Eleven

Nathan barely slept that night, and when he did sleep he dreamed about the ratings and Karl and Suki all on Mars. He woke up miserable and tired, as if he hadn't dozed at all.

The next three days were torture. Even though the classes were interesting, he couldn't stay focused on the material. All he thought about were the ratings. Or the fact that for the first time in his life he could lose. He had never been so scared. And so when the ratings were posted Friday morning, it was almost a relief.

Until he saw where they were ranked, which was at the bottom of the last quarter.

"That's impossible," Gen said flatly. "I know that Kovi Oldjai's team didn't do nearly as well on the astronomy test, and they're way ahead of us."

Alice was nearly in tears, and even Noemi was subdued. Only Karl seemed unaffected. "It's fair," he said over breakfast. "We've got ten times as many demerits as anyone else."

Lanie didn't say a word. She just sat as her eggs got cold, her hands jammed deep into the pockets of her jacket. Nathan wasn't even sure she was aware the rest of them were there until she spoke.

"You know," she said just as they were all ready to leave, "you know, I'd like to take a look myself at that rating business. Go over the trace too."

"You mean you think someone tampered with the computer?" Sergei asked, aghast.

Lanie shrugged. "I don't know. Maybe they did. And even if no one did, maybe I can fix it."

"What do you mean, fix it?" Karl demanded, his face reddening. "You mean cheat, you mean lie, and we'll get caught and thrown out. You don't belong in this program. You belong in juvenile hall."

"Well, I think we should at least check the possibility that someone else has been tampering," Alice said evenly. "If we can."

Lanie smiled secretly. "Oh, I can. Don't worry about that. No problem."

"This is immoral," Karl protested.

"We're not talking about changing anything," Nathan told him firmly. "We're just checking to see that no one else did either."

"But how could someone change our ranking if they didn't have our password?" Sergei asked innocently. "The only people who have it is us and Dr. Thompson."

Nathan saw Alice, Sergei, and Lanie give Karl a hard look. Karl only sneered again, as usual. Nathan was getting tired of his attitude. Enough was enough. "Let's vote on it now. Who's in favor of Lanie taking a look?"

Everyone voted yes except Karl. Which was also to be expected. They agreed that Lanie would report back to them by Monday breakfast. That should give her enough time.

The weekend dragged by. They did the usual weekend things, going out in Houston's all-too-warm November weather to the wilder shops on Montrose, looking for used CDs and amusement. They went to the Galleria, the giant mall with the ice skating rink in the middle, and Sergei tried to teach the rest of them to skate. He was not completely successful. Gen and Nathan did well enough, Lanie had skated before, but Noemi was hopeless. She couldn't even stand on the blades.

One good thing about going to Houston with Noemi's credit cards was that they could buy things they needed for the vehicle. Between Radio Shack and the hardware store, they managed to collect enough lightweight aluminum for the frame, and the electronics and batteries to drive it without attracting attention in the center. Other teams were preparing, too, but everyone had ideas about what they were doing from what they had requested from supply.

Nathan got so involved in the project that he forgot about tracing any tampering with the computer. Or maybe he wanted to forget, had forced the whole thing from his mind.

Sunday morning Lanie asked Nathan if he'd come with her and bring a wire coat hanger. Alice was along also, presumably to play guard. Lanie led them to Dr. Thompson's office on the second floor of one of the buildings around the fountain. No one was around. Even the most dedicated were still sleeping or out eating pancakes.

"Here," she whispered.

Nathan cursed under his breath. He wasn't used to

117

breaking locks. The only time he had ever done this before was when he had locked his keys in the house and his mother wasn't going to be home from work for hours. And it was January and they had been sent home early because of the blizzard warnings. Even then he had always assumed that Mrs. Anderson next door would let him stay until his mother got home. It was Mrs. Anderson's brother who brought the coat hanger and showed Nathan how to pick the lock.

Now his palms were sweaty and slipped on the wire. He twisted and turned it and didn't feel it catch. "What happens if we don't get in?" he asked urgently, wiggling the homemade lock pick desperately.

"We try the window," Lanie said reasonably. "People don't usually lock their windows. And if they did, we can try a slim-jim."

Nathan groaned and tried the wire again. This time he felt something and the door sprang open. He was rewarded by a bright smile from Lanie and a nod from Alice. They followed Lanie into the office and closed the door. Then, while Lanie went to the terminal, Alice and Nathan sat almost with their ears against the door. There was no sound in the corridor at all.

Nathan's heart was pounding so loud that he was certain it could be heard in security. Below he could hear the usual chatter of the tourists as they wandered into this enclave, where they were explicitly not allowed. Lanie cursed a few times and then whistled.

Nathan found himself counting the seconds and holding his breath. The moment lingered forever, and then Lanie tapped him on the shoulder and signaled them to leave.

The hardest thing was not to run. Nathan wanted to

get away from that office as quickly as possible, but Lanie held his belt. "Don't," she warned. "It's more suspicious."

Nathan swallowed and kept walking. He wasn't sure he didn't agree with Karl at that point. He wondered why Lanie had chosen him instead of Gen, who probably knew as much about picking locks and probably would have enjoyed their little adventure.

The three teammates blended in with the busload of tourists for a few moments, wandering around and listening to their uninformed comments. As they broke off from the tour group to leave the quadrangle, they were intercepted by no one less than Suki Long herself.

She came out between the buildings as the bus group faded down the hill, and she simply stood there, not smiling. "I hope you have found what you want," she said softly when they were close enough.

Nathan was furious. He was ready to explode, to pick up Little Miss Perfect and shake her until her teeth rattled. But to his surprise it was Alice who beat him out. "Why are you always after us?" Alice asked in fury. "Why don't you bother someone else? Or are you afraid of the competition and you're trying to psych us out?"

Suki Long only smiled enigmatically. "I just want to check on how you're doing. We're supposed to be concerned with the welfare of others, aren't we?" She looked right at Lanie when she said that and Nathan was afraid that Lanie would slit the other girl's throat. But Lanie only spat on the ground and walked on.

Nathan and Alice followed Lanie's example, ignoring Suki Long and her feeble attempt to intimidate them. Nathan was burning with both anger and curiosity by the time they returned to the dorm, but had waited before he spoke. Now he couldn't wait any longer. He turned to Lanie. "Well?" he demanded.

She shook her head and led them inside. Instead of going to the TV room, they went downstairs to one of the practice rooms next to the laundry. There were four rooms down there, each soundproofed and equipped with music stands, outlets, and other odd bits of paraphernalia. Technically the rooms were for members of the space center orchestra, but everyone used them. Gen was one of the most frequent visitors to the dorm's catacombs.

When they arrived in Gen's favorite practice room, the others were already assembled. Even Karl stood contemptuously in the corner. Nathan and Alice joined them, facing Lanie and waiting for her report.

Lanie took a deep breath. "It's very strange," she began. "I couldn't find any hint of tampering. Nothing at all. But then I got a little deeper and got into the files and asked for a rank list from the closed data. And guess what, guys? We're number seven on the list. That strike you as strange?"

"But we were number seven from the bottom of the list," Gen pointed out unhappily. "Could you have just gotten it wrong?"

"No way," Lanie insisted. "There's something funny about this whole business. I think we should confront Dr. Thompson and get a few straight answers."

"Then we'll have to admit to breaking into his office, getting into restricted files, and questioning the listing," Karl droned. "You want to do that?"

"No, not necessarily," Nathan said, a pattern forming in his mind. "But I don't think that confrontation is the best strategy right now. There's something else to this

120

whole thing, I think. I can't see it clearly, but I know something else is involved."

"Oh, now we're giving up science for funny feelings," Karl said. "What next? Do we cut up a goat and study its entrails? Or are we going to try to mix up a witch's flying potion?"

Karl's outburst didn't make Nathan angry. He'd been expecting it. Karl's bad attitude was only boring now, and predictable. He didn't even care, and certainly couldn't be bothered.

"No, wait. I can almost see it," Nathan said. "I just need a little time."

Part IV: December

Chapter Twelve

The first week of December was in the eighties, which was just one more thing that was wrong about it. For the others, well, since the ratings had been posted, they had been ignored by the rest of the candidates. The way he had always treated the geeks and dummies, Nathan reflected. Now he was one.

Nathan's mind was so involved with his own team's problems that he didn't get particularly excited about the survival trek. Even now in the theater, surrounded by the thrilled buzz of conversation, he was lost in thought. If only he could break through. He knew it, bits of it, and yet the whole still eluded him. And so he missed the beginning of the presentation. As a matter of fact, it wasn't until Gen poked him in the ribs that he even paid attention to the speaker.

Dr. Jonathan Herrin was in charge of environmental factors. They had studied in his class for three months so far, learning about such things as forestation and how plants help create oxygen, about how to find shelter and how to travel in a desert, and even basic first aid and how to make flint knives. It was a crazy hodgepodge course and no one had taken it as seriously as formal mathematics or chemistry. Nathan had always considered it a fun break.

The funniest time had been when they were working on making stone knives and tools. Dr. Herrin had brought in an archaeologist, who had explained about hammer stones and pressure flaking and shown them examples of finished work. Then they had taken what looked like plain gray stone and began to bang it up. At least that's what it seemed like. All very silly and childish, Suki Long had said in her superior way. A waste of time.

They had made crude knives and then, in fun, Mario DelVecchio had tested his blade against his thumb. And had cut himself almost to the bone. He had stayed there, stock still, watching the blood come out of his hand, more amazed that the primitive tool was effective than anything else.

"Take him to the health center," the archaeologist had said. "Now you know that primitive doesn't necessarily mean inferior. An obsidian blade is as sharp as anything we can make today. It's just extremely brittle. But obsidian is still used in making special surgical tools, just the way the Aztec did six hundred years ago."

"What's obsidian?" Nathan had whispered over to Sergei, who had already begun his geology specialization.

"Volcanic glass," Sergei had explained.

But everyone saw the survival trek as a game, not an exercise in techniques they would need once they arrived on the red planet. Really, Nathan was counting on the higher technology of Gen's vehicle rather than flint knives.

Actually, Nathan was convinced that it was more tradition than anything else. In the earliest days of the space program, before they had controlled landings, astronauts were trained to survive in various environments in case they came down in a desert by mistake, or in a jungle. They had even had to eat snake on at least one occasion.

When Nathan told Noemi about that, she immediately told Dr. Thompson that she absolutely refused to eat snake. Their supervisor replied that if anyone asked *him* to eat snake, he would resign from the program. There were a few things in life that he was just not prepared to do. Noemi was not the only team member who was very relieved.

So there they were, getting ready for the famous survival trek. Sitting in the theater, looking at slides of different plants. Some were edible and some were dangerous and some were medicinal. Nathan did not take notes. With Gen's and Noemi's memories, someone would know the right stuff if it came along. He had a hard enough time telling the weeds from the tomatoes in the garden until the fruit came in.

The whole thing was pointless as far as Nathan could see. After all, where they had to survive there wouldn't be any plants. There wouldn't even be a breatheable atmosphere.

Well, they had until that night to prepare, and whatever they could carry in their packs. "Swiss Army knife," Alice said immediately. "Flashlights. And a good rope."

"Why do we need a rope?" Noemi asked, genuinely puzzled.

"You never know when one comes in handy," Alice

replied.

"And as many Mylar blankets as we can get," Nathan interjected. He had more than one reason to be glad for the ultralight, thin plastic blankets coated with reflective glaze. It really did keep people warm although it went against intuition that it would. "We can use them for tents and rain ponchos too."

"And I'll bring the Walkman," Gen offered.

Sergei balked. "For what?" he demanded.

Gen looked surprised. "For the radio, of course. We can at least get the weather and maybe even the location."

"I'll bring my credit cards," Noemi stated.

Nathan had to stifle the urge to laugh. He knew that Noemi was trying to be practical and just didn't have very much experience. A lot of good credit cards were going to do on Mars. Being rich wasn't going to help anyone there. But he didn't want to dissuade her, so he let it go.

"What about a compass and a map?" Karl asked. He still wasn't happy in the group, but he had to go along on the trek too, and Nathan was certain that he didn't want to stay out in the wild any longer than necessary. If for nothing else, it was uncomfortable.

"Good," Sergei agreed. "And water purification tablets and first aid kit and aspirin."

"Where are you going to find water purification tablets?" Lanie asked.

Sergei smiled. "I have a bottle with me. In case the water in Houston didn't agree with me."

Nathan interrupted them. "Let's get to work on it," he hurried them along. "We have only until dinner, and it's three-thirty already. I suggest that Noemi take Alice

126

and Sergei on an expedition to the Galleria to get whatever we need there. Karl and I can get the Mylar blankets at the tourist concession stand right here. Gen has to get the vehicle frame broken down into parts that we can carry."

"Already done," Gen said, his eyes twinkling. "Extremely lightweight and durable, and the electronics are all sorted out and packed."

"And what do I do?" Lanie asked.

"You don't go shoplifting," Karl said dryly.

Lanie stuck out her tongue at him. This was getting ridiculous. "Look, we don't have any time," Nathan said. "Lanie, you're in charge of getting everything into our clothing and pockets without us getting caught. Okay?"

This time she smiled. Even Karl had to agree. No reason not to find a good way to use ability, even when it was acquired doing something wrong. Nathan sort of felt sorry for Lanie and didn't at the same time. But he knew that her skills would be useful in the long run. Someone who had managed to break into the school computer had brains and guts, both of which were going to mean a lot come Mars.

Dinner was unusually good that night. Maybe the dietetic staff had decided that they needed to eat well before going off for who knew how long. The point of the trek was to make their way back to the base from a deserted area. The first team in won extra points, but to come in at all was a way to win. Each team had a quarter to call in if by the end of forty-eight hours they still had not returned.

They had barbecued chicken and ribs, cole slaw, and French fries followed by brownies. Lanie took seconds and thirds and stuffed them into her pockets, and told the others to do the same. They should be able to find food along the way somehow, but it was better to carry some supply. Packs carefully filled with necessities and pieces of the vehicle wrapped in towels, the team presented themselves to the theater once again.

This time there were no lectures and no slides. They just waited until Dr. Thompson called out their names. Then they came forward and were led to a van by one of the security guards. There they were blindfolded and the van took off.

Unable to see, Nathan couldn't judge the time. He tried to memorize the route at first, having seen something like that in a James Bond movie, but there were a lot of turns. He thought the driver was making a special effort to disorient them, and it was working.

It felt as if they were driving for hours. No one talked. There had to be at least two other teams in the van, but with the blindfolds no one wanted to break the silence. They were waiting. The van stopped and people were let off. Not their team. Nathan wondered whether the others were going to be closer to their final destination than his own group. That made him angry. The van took off once again, more turns and craziness until another group was let out. It seemed as if they drove ages longer to the place where the driver finally told them to remove their blindfolds and leave the van.

It was the middle of nowhere. Not even the surface of Mars could look so deserted. The van roared off, its lights the last sign of civilization they saw. There wasn't a light, a house, or the sound of a car anywhere.

And it was terribly dark. Nathan looked up and scanned the sky. He had thought the forecast was for a clear night, but he couldn't see many stars. And they were far enough from the city so that he should have been able to. No, there had to be some cloud cover, which meant there might be rain. Great. "Well," he told himself, "you always wanted to have adventures."

Karl must have overheard and snorted. "My father always said that on a real adventure you were usually tired, cold, hungry, thirsty and had to use the bathroom."

"You know, you're a real killjoy," Gen said. "This should be fun. You know, we just hang out and have a good time and put together this invention which you get to drive and roll out in a dune buggy. Like in the movies. Noemi's even dressed for it."

Noemi smiled. "At least these can be seen in the dark," she said, thumbs under her hot pink suspenders.

"Yeah, right, we're going to use her for the rear reflector," Lanie said.

"Stop bitching and get out the compass and let's get going," Alice said firmly, always the practical one.

Between the compass and the map they were able to tell very little about where they were in relation to the Johnson Space Center. They couldn't see the hazy light from the city to even get a general direction, and they didn't know where they'd come from. The stars weren't much help either, with the cloud cover. Nathan cursed under his breath. He'd been planning on showing them all his brilliant navigational skills, finding and following the stars to where they looked right from outside the dorm. He hadn't planned on clouds.

"Let's get the dune buggy assembled," Gen said. He unrolled his towels and began fitting parts together.

It was a wonderful contraption, Nathan had to admit. The lightweight frame was low and broad enough to carry all seven of them and their equipment. It worked on tank tracks, not wheels, to take into account all terrain, and how Gen had managed to come up with a set of bearings that could be fit together and taken apart so easily was something that amazed Nathan.

"We'll win more points than anyone on that alone," he said.

Gen smiled. "All aboard." And Karl threw the switch.

The buggy jolted forward and shuddered. Karl gripped the steering contraption and Nathan felt his teeth rattle. They were rolling! Karl looked happier than he had since he was at the wheel of the Mercedes, and Gen was yelling something in Japanese, his long hair flying in the wind.

They were going to win. No doubt about that. *Put that on your plate and eat it, Suki Long,* Nathan thought with pleasure. He could feel winning in his blood. Mars was closer than ever.

Suddenly the buggy jolted to a halt. He looked at Karl, wondering why he had stopped, but Karl was already turning to Gen.

"Something's wrong," the German boy said carefully. "We've lost our power."

"No power?" Gen asked, puzzled.

"Well, let's check it out," Nathan said. He had to say something. Gen looked stricken, as if he personally had let them all down. "Maybe it's just that a connection came loose driving or something. This isn't the best road."

They went over the entire vehicle in the dark. The frame, the wires, the connections, the wheels, and it

130

was all perfect. Until they reached the battery. It was bone dry.

"But it was fine when I bought it," Gen protested. "I checked it and stored it away, and it was new. This can't happen all by itself."

Lanie elbowed her way through the boys and inspected the battery under the beam of her heavy-duty flashlight. "Yeah," she said, "that was drained, all right. I used to know kids who did this kind of stuff. Someone sabotaged us, no question about that."

"But who'd do that?" Noemi asked.

They all looked at Karl. "No," he said firmly. "I really wanted to drive that buggy. Maybe one of you did it because you didn't want me to drive."

"No," Nathan said, frowning. "None of us would do this. But Karl, you talked about it, didn't you? You told Suki and Dale and those guys about what we were building, didn't you?"

"I had to protect my reputation," Karl protested angrily. "They all called our team a joke. I had to tell them something. I was defending us."

"My design. My beautiful design," Gen mourned. He didn't look at the others, just kept nudging the drained battery.

"So what do we do now?" Noemi asked, wringing her hands, her pearl white nails glittering in the dark.

"We walk," Lanie said without hesitation. "Staying here won't do us any good at all. And there's this dirt road the van took. We backtrack until we get to a highway. And there's got to be a sign on the highway somewhere to tell us where we are."

It was the best plan they'd heard, and so they began to walk. It wasn't bad once you got into it, Nathan thought. The evening was warm and the ground was hard and level and he was wearing a sturdy pair of hightops. The walking was even pleasant.

Sergei pulled out the compass when they got to the paved road. The road itself ran east-west, which meant they had only two choices instead of four. "We're more likely to find somebody, or a sign or something, if we stay on the road," Gen kept insisting, although Nathan, Alice, and Sergei were all in favor of striking out across the open land.

"You know, this is ridiculous," Karl insisted. "Why don't we just go to sleep, and when we wake up we'll have a much better idea of where we are. And then we can get back. I'm tired."

Nathan just ignored him and began walking east. It seemed the most sensible thing. Besides, if he remembered the map correctly, they'd hit either Houston or the Gulf of Mexico. One way or the other there was something. Not the open wildness of the heartland of Texas.

Noemi fell to the back of the pack and had a hard time keeping up. Although she had worn her sneakers this time, she still wasn't as strong as the others. Even working hard at the gym and track hadn't gotten her quite caught up. Nathan felt sorry for her and dropped back to encourage her. She was breathing hard. But it was obvious that she was walking with Gen, trying to keep him company and be there in case he needed a friend.

Gen was totally miserable. Nathan could hardly stand to think about how he must have felt. All those hours, all that work on something, only to have it destroyed by someone who was jealous. Perhaps if he had made a mistake it wouldn't have been so bad. You had to take the heat for your own garbage. But this was the worst possible thing. And it was so unfair!

As a distraction, and because his walking had fallen into a rhythm, Nathan began to whistle.

Pretty soon Alice and Karl had picked up the tune and changed it into cancan music. Lanie even began to kick and skip as she walked. Sergei joined in whistling, but the notes he hit bore no relationship to the melody. Karl complained that Sergei was hurting his ears, which made Noemi giggle. Frankly Nathan had to agree. He proposed that they make the first Martian law immediately, and that it would be that tone-deaf people would keep quiet.

Sergei protested loudly, and started singing at the top of his voice. Whereupon Alice, Nathan, and Lanie tried to drown him out. This was even worse than the whistling, and Noemi was laughing so hard that she was breathing in fierce gasps. Even Gen could not resist, and the laughter caught up with him too.

They didn't notice the unnatural stillness for a long time. Even the smell of the Gulf crept up on them stealthily. But the quiet was part of the dark, embedded in the night. Their singing, their laughter, their games, had been a cheerful protest against the sullen dark.

And then the wind became furious.

Chapter Thirteen

Nathan, Lanie, and Alice faced into the coming storm and began to dance with it, exhilarated by the whipping wind and the heavy smell of rain. Karl held back and Sergei helped Noemi find a place to sit in the grass-covered sand. Only Gen seemed worried, casting an exploratory glance over the scene.

A brilliant, jagged bolt of lightning lit the scene like daylight, and for an instant the entire group could make out a structure silhouetted against the sky. The thunder crash went right through them, shaking them to the core. No discussion was needed for them all to dash to the structure as the first thick drops began to fall with the force of hail.

The shelter turned out to be a squat abandoned gas station. The white stucco had gone dark with age and leakage and it smelled of damp and decay. But it was shelter and they were glad of it when the rain started belting down in sheets.

"I'm glad we're in here," Noemi said as another thunderclap shook them through. "I'm surprised they'd send us out with a storm like this coming on, though."

Sergei laughed and touched her shoulder. "Weather prediction is not a science, no matter what anyone says. We could use the *I Ching* and it would be as accurate."

"We're lucky to have found this place," Alice said. "Walking around in the open could be dangerous with the lightning, and I think I noticed a lightning rod on this place. We should be safe."

Gen blinked and nodded. "Then God has saved us all," he said. "If we had been riding in that aluminum buggy out in this weather . . ." He didn't have to say any more. The metal would have attracted lightning like honey attracts flies.

It was difficult to hear over the roar of the storm, and there were no lights. Nathan turned on one of the flashlights, and they had a brief glimpse of their environment. Too filled with dirt, rags, and discarded newspapers for a fire to be safe. And they agreed to use only one flashlight at a time. No matter how new they were, the team couldn't afford to waste the batteries and bulbs.

The whole situation made Nathan light-headed. "You know," he said, "I think we should all tell ghost stories or something. 'It was a dark and stormy night . . .' Stuff like that. 'Quoth the raven, nevermore.' "

"What was that?" Karl asked.

"Edgar Allan Poe," Nathan replied immediately.

"Not that, jerk. That sound outside. Didn't you hear it?"

Nathan had thought it was just thunder again, another loud crashing sound in the dark. Now he realized it had a metallic tone to it, something different from the storm. Something not quite so alive and natural. Something frightening.

He went to the door immediately and was out in the rain again. A car had skidded on the slick pavement and gone headfirst into a telephone pole. "Come on," he said, but he didn't look back.

Nathan felt more than a little nervous approaching the car. He'd seen all the scare movies in driver's ed and was sure he didn't want to know what the survivors looked like. If there were survivors. Maybe all the people in the car were dead.

That was the way it was on TV. He'd seen plenty of accidents on TV too. He was afraid of what he would find, and afraid of how he would react. But there wasn't any choice. There must have been people in that car, and he didn't see anyone moving.

He forced himself forward, bent almost double against the wind and rain. He couldn't see the ground in front of his feet, but it slipped under him and he sprawled in the mud. Getting up was hard. Making himself go on to the wrecked car was worse. The smell of gasoline was light under the heavy rain, but as he approached he could detect it and it was even more frightening than what could possibly be in that car.

He braced himself and pulled the driver's door open. There was a figure strapped into the seat, not moving. Nathan wanted to throw up. Instead, he forced himself to unbuckle the seat belt and pull the stranger under the shoulders, dragging him from the car. At least the body was warm, and Nathan prayed there was a pulse.

As he felt for the carotid artery in the neck, he was able to make out the victim's face. It was someone he knew. More than that, it was another candidate. It was Vikram Singh from Suki Long's group. What was he doing driving a car on the survival trek in this storm?

Somehow the fact that he knew who it was steadied Nathan. He became confident, his fingers moving firmly over the throat to find a faint but discernible pulse. Silently he thanked God and started to drag Vikram toward the shelter. One move at a time, one thing following another logically. He thought he was organized and didn't realize that panic had already outrun his mind and he was functioning on instinct.

Over by the car there were other shadows moving and more noise. Nathan held his breath. Something about them reminded him of every horror movie he had ever seen. For one terrible minute he wondered if it really was possible for the dead to be reanimated and come mindlessly after the living. Then he took a ragged breath and forced his mind to stop jabbering in terror.

He looked at the car again and realized that Gen, Sergei, and Alice were pulling someone from the passenger side. *See, that was stupid,* he told himself firmly. They were shouting something at him, at one another, but the rain drowned out the words.

The doorway was just behind him, and he was already under the tiny overhang that protected his face from the worst of the pelting rain. He glanced up and saw Karl standing frozen in the doorway, his face an unnatural white and his fists clenched.

There wasn't any time for Karl's nonsense, Nathan thought with exasperation. He yelled again, ordering Karl out of the way.

Karl didn't seem to hear him. The boy just stood there as if he himself were already dead and a statue. Nathan had the urge to slap his face and make him come back to reality when an immense bolt of lightning did it for him.

The lightning was very close that time, and backlit the scene so brilliantly that it hurt Nathan's eyes. But in that flash he had seen something else, a form on the ground a little way from the car that he hadn't seen before. And he was sure no one else had.

"Here," he said roughly, dragging Vikram's still form up to Karl's hands. "You take care of him. There's someone else still out there."

Karl looked strange and glittery in the dark. For a moment Nathan had the impression that he was crying. But that was crazy. It was probably the rain.

He went back to where he thought he had seen the other body. He approached what seemed to be a human shape on the ground, and for a moment hoped that it might be a hunk of the telephone pole. He reached down and found cool flesh, yielding and soft and dangerous.

He pulled the body around until he could check the breathing and pulse. It was a girl. Automatically he made sure she was still alive. His hands were coated with something thick and sticky. Mud, he supposed. He looked at the girl again and suddenly he recognized her.

Hurt and unconscious, Suki Long was simply very vulnerable and pretty. None of the competitive, razor-voiced snobbery tightened her features. Nathan was surprised. He was even more surprised when he picked her up and found out that she was tiny and light. She had always seemed so large because of her dominating personality.

He carried her into the gas station, where Lanie had already set up a makeshift first aid station. When he brought Suki over she gasped. "She's bleeding badly,"

Lanie said, playing a flashlight over Suki's form. Nathan looked down at his hands. With the flashlight he could see they were covered with blood.

"Direct pressure," Noemi said in a businesslike manner, and took a gauze bandage and began to press down on it. Noemi, for all her ditzy behavior, now was acting like a real trouper. It was Karl who was coming unglued.

He sat crumpled in the corner, his shoulders heaving. Noemi taking care of his burden, Nathan was free to join the one teammate who had never seemed to care very much for them.

He laid a hand on Karl's shoulder, and for the first time Karl didn't jerk away. "You okay, man?" Nathan asked feebly.

Karl shook his head, and his sobbing didn't stop. "I don't care, I don't," he said fiercely.

Nathan didn't believe him. He didn't know what to make of Karl's strange behavior, but he knew that Karl cared. Maybe he cared too much.

He got up and started to turn away when Karl grabbed his arm. "I didn't want her to die. I didn't, really I didn't. But I couldn't help thinking about it sometimes, you know, when she didn't want me to do something. I didn't mean it."

"Who?" Gen asked gently. Nathan hadn't seen him come up behind, and the question startled him.

"Who didn't you want to die?" Gen repeated his question. "Not Suki. Suki isn't dead. She's unconscious, but she isn't dead. She's going to be okay."

Karl shook his head almost violently. *"Mutti,"* he whispered. "My mother, after the accident. Just like this, a storm at Christmastime, and I didn't want it to happen, I swear."

And suddenly Nathan understood everything. He remembered when his parents had divorced, how he had thought he was somehow responsible and had been a loner for a long time. He pushed friends away because he felt cursed in some way, as if bad luck followed him around. If it didn't, his dad would still be home, right?

He'd been a lot younger than Karl. He thought that now these things were easier to deal with. But maybe not entirely. And death was much worse than a divorce. At least he saw his dad for a couple of weeks every summer.

And that was going to change, he realized. He would never go to his dad's for the summer again once they left Earth. He would never see his father, or his mother either. It would be final, as if they had died, and suddenly Nathan felt abandoned.

"You guys must really hate me," Karl said, looking up. He wasn't crying anymore; the moment had passed. But instead of his usual sneer his face was open, and Nathan knew that Karl had been trying to be horrible to hurt himself, not the team.

"No," Gen said. "Even I don't hate you, and I should after the way you told those guys how to trash my buggy. But, what the hey, there aren't that many of us. We can't afford to hate one another."

"Look, Karl, there wasn't anything you could do to help your mother," Nathan said carefully. "But you can do something now. You can help us take care of Suki and her friends. So let's move."

"Yeah. We're miles from anywhere and they trashed the car," Lanie said, frustration coloring her voice. "What they were doing away from the rest of their team

140

and in that car I won't even begin to guess. But anyway, how do we get them to a doctor? Carry them? We could make a litter like we did in that primitive stuff class, but we don't have anything strong enough to lay them on. The space blankets'll tear."

"At least the rain has stopped," Alice pointed out.

"We shouldn't move them anyway," Sergei pointed out. "They need an ambulance."

"Great. And how are we going to get one here? Materialize it?" Gen asked haphazardly.

"No, silly, use the telephone." Noemi spoke as if to kindergarten students.

"Have you noticed that there isn't a telephone?" Karl said.

Noemi just shrugged. "There's a line. All we have to do is tap in, and they'll get out here fast enough. If nothing else, to stop us from using the phone without paying. And if we need it, I do have my calling card."

And it wasn't a bad idea, either, Nathan thought. Noemi wasn't really as silly as she seemed. He was now convinced of that. He wandered out to take a look at the telephone line. If it was live, it would be dangerous.

When the car had hit the pole it had pulled the wire and brought it down. That much was good. At least they didn't have to climb. But it was lying there like so much dead cable. From a safe distance Sergei threw an empty Coke can at it and hit the exposed end. Nothing happened at all.

"Dead," he said, shaking his head. "What now?"

Chapter Fourteen

"They don't seem to be doing very well," Noemi said.

Alice came over and took a look. "Suki's still bleeding," she noticed. "It must be worse than we thought." Alice looked Noemi up and down. "Give me your suspenders," she told her teammate.

Noemi blinked and hesitated.

"For a tourniquet," she explained. "They're elastic. That'll help."

Noemi unfastened what had been a frivolous fashion item and handed it wordlessly to Alice. The farm girl immediately had the pink elastic wrapped hard around Suki's leg.

"We've got to get help," Gen said.

Nathan nodded miserably. Frightened and wishing it were all just a bad dream, he stepped outside and looked at the sky. Now that the flash storm had gone, the atmosphere was clean. He could see the stars and picked out Sirius low on the horizon. He remembered that the telescope for the astronomy class he had been taking at the University of Houston was trained on Sirius for the next hour. How he wished he could leap up and the astronomers could see him.

Of course that was totally stupid. Like knowing there were radio waves all around, it didn't make the situation easier. In fact, it made it harder. Knowing that there was a telescope pointed in their direction but there was no way to tell his friends at the university made him feel even more lonely and abandoned.

Karl was already going through the trunk of the smashed car, muttering to himself.

"Hey, wait, won't that blow up?" Alice asked.

"Only on television," Karl answered. "Don't worry. Maybe they had a flare. We have to signal somehow."

Lanie joined Karl in searching the car. "You're right," she said briskly. "Let's find something to signal."

Nathan didn't join in the hunt. A flare was too weak to be seen for any distance. Maybe it was something to do, but it didn't seem to have a lot of practical value.

Karl came back waving three pink flares in his hand.

"You know, maybe I could get the car running," Gen said. "Wrap them up real good and take them to a hospital. I bet I can fix the car in a few hours."

"We don't have a few hours," Alice said. "Suki's in shock and she needs help *now*."

"Maybe we should start a fire and someone would see it from far away and come check it out," Sergei said.

"Yeah, like maybe with the university telescope," Nathan said. "Only they'd never notice a little fire on the ground."

"Huh?" Lanie asked. "Why are you talking about the university telescope?"

"They're doing the readings on Sirius, remember?" Nathan said. "I keep thinking there must be a way to signal them. Like blow up this gas station or something."

Lanie tapped the flare on the ground. "You know, if we tossed this high enough so they could see it, I bet they'd come looking for us real fast."

"And you're Hercules," Alice said. "How are you going to 'toss' it up high enough?"

"Maybe a rocket, a rocket could do it," Karl said.

"Where are we going to get a *rocket?*" Noemi asked.

"Wait, no, it's great," Nathan said, excitement catching. "Goddard's first rocket wasn't much. They aren't hard to build as long as we have some fuel. And something to compress it."

He took out the spare flashlight and began to dig through the rubble of the abandoned station. Yes, mixed in with the rags and old newspapers he found what he had been looking for—a tube from a roll of paper towels. Amazing how useful some things were. He dug it out and put it on his lap.

Alice, with Noemi's help, was checking over Suki, Vikram, and Leon. "Bleeding, breathing, broken bones," she recited from the Red Cross manual. "After bleeding we have to worry about shock. More accident victims die of shock than of bleeding."

Sergei unrolled the Mylar blankets and wrapped them around the injured teammates. Alice nodded. "Right. You have to keep shock victims warm. And

144

give them water if they're conscious."

Karl and Lanie joined in the search. The rest of what they needed for the plan he hoped to find in the car, but that didn't mean that the packing wasn't all there. After all, rags and papers soaked in gasoline might just work. He didn't know if it would burn hot enough for his purposes, and they'd have to keep the energy contained.

It was Lanie who found the matches settled in the dust under the counter, the big wooden safety kind. She held them up like a trophy. "Look, fuel," she announced.

"Well, that'll work," Karl agreed. "Which is certainly better than nothing at all. So we have a tube to contain the explosion and fuel. And the flare. We need something to line the tube to contain the explosion and then we need something to keep the flare up long enough."

Nathan held up a finger and then threw an empty Coke can in front of them.

"No, too heavy," Karl said suddenly. And then his face lit up with a sudden inspiration. "But I bet I know where we can find a lot of chewing gum. Suki doesn't go anywhere without chewing gum."

"What does chewing gum have to do with anything?" Lanie asked.

"The foil wrappers," Nathan said, the light dawning. "We line the tube with foil wrappers that will reflect the energy of the explosion back inside so that it's almost completely controlled. Fully directional."

Lanie shook her head but smiled at the same time. "Remember that Saturn V outside the space center?"

145

she asked. "Just like that, huh? Only smaller."

It was Alice who found the ten-pack of Beech-Nut in Suki's pocket.

"How're we going to attach the foil to the inside of the tube?" Noemi asked naively.

Gen smiled evilly. "With the chewing gum, of course." He took a pack from Karl, unwrapped all five sticks of gum, and began chewing them all.

Alice shook her head. "If we're going to use the gum to attach to foil, then we have to chew each piece separately."

"Then you do it," Nathan said, throwing her the pack. He had something else to do. The Coke can was too heavy to use to line the booster, but it was still necessary equipment. With the can opener attachment on Alice's Swiss Army knife he took off the top where the flip tab had been opened.

Sergei watched very carefully and nodded. He took a piece of rope and brought it to the car. He siphoned off some gas into the bottom of the can and soaked a length of rope in it. Lanie complimented him on his siphoning technique while chewing a large wad of gum.

Inside, Noemi was now using the knife to cut off the match heads. She had a good pile going, and then they were finished lining the tube with foil she had enough matches cut to fill the entire bottom section. Then Nathan used the opener again to make the can top small enough to fit snugly inside the upper part of the cardboard tube. He ran a bit of the rope through the tab opening down to where the matches were and up to where the flare was going to go. The rope wouldn't tie on to the lighting end of the flare, so he coiled them together to make a fuse that would light once the rocket was airborne.

Then he took out the last Mylar blanket and spread it out. With four long pieces of wire scavenged from the car's electrical system he attached the blanket to the flare. Then he folded the whole thing together carefully and packed it as the booster's payload.

"What's the blanket for?" Noemi asked.

"Parachute," Sergei answered.

"But why do we need one?"

"We want to keep the flare as high as possible as long as possible," Nathan answered. "The wire is long enough to keep the flare from melting the plastic when it goes off. So it should work."

But Noemi wasn't listening anymore. Instead, she was studying their handiwork. "You know, something bothers me. What about guidance and stabilization? This could just blow any way at all, and we want it to go pretty much straight up."

Nathan blinked. He hadn't thought about that, and Noemi was right. Trust the theoretical types. The only useful things they knew to tell you was why things wouldn't work.

It was Lanie who picked up the remaining cuplike part of the Coke can and rotated it in her hand. "Hmmm" was all she said. Then she picked out the can opener attachment on the knife. "Cut four triangles out of this," she said, drawing the long triangles with her finger.

Karl nodded at her with respect and began to cut

as Gen asked what for. "Fins," Lanie said. "The curve of the can, here, will give the rocket a spin that will act to stabilize it so we can get the maximum trajectory."

Nathan whistled low. He was impressed. And he was proud of them. His team, all of them. Whether or not they were selected, he knew that they were special. Not just smart, even brilliant, but brave and resourceful too.

When the fins were cut out, Gen cut places for them on the outside of the tube and stuck the ragged pieces through. "Little loose," he muttered.

Karl pulled out yet one more pack of gum. This, however, was different from the others. It wasn't double wrapped with the foil liner, but with bright pink waxed paper. "I didn't know that this would come in handy," he said, and popped a piece into his mouth.

Then they set the assembly up well outside the shelter, over the worst of the mud, where there was nothing to catch fire. From a distance it looked like a respectable, if homemade, rocket. It even rather reminded Nathan of pictures he had seen of Robert Goddard, the father of modern rockets, with his own early experimental models.

He lit the end of the rope he had fastened as a fuse to the innards of the booster and watched it burn. He felt a knot in his stomach as the flame approached the little rocket and held his breath as it caught. Something could go wrong. It could explode right there. It could—but it didn't. Just like the Saturn V, its reflected controlled explosion lifted it off the base and straight into the sky.

148

Lanie was right about the spin. Nathan could see it going around so fast that it flew straight and true. There was a massive flash as the booster was eaten up by flames and the fuse for the flare lit. Fast and true and high, he could see it around them, the bright pink flare reflected down under the Mylar parachute.

He let out his breath raggedly. It had worked. They had done it, the whole team together. And they had done it well.

But when he went back inside the station he realized that their accomplishment wouldn't mean anything if it didn't bring help fast. Lanie and Sergei were holding flashlights on their wounded competition. Suki, Vikram, and Leon did not look good. All of them had an ashen cast to their very differently colored complexions.

"Blue shock," Alice said softly. "We should raise their legs."

Sergei moved immediately to prop the victims' feet on the lower shelf of the partially destroyed counter. "They don't feel right," he said.

Nathan moved over and touched Vikram's hand. Sergei was right. The skin was cool and rubbery. He looked more closely and saw that their breathing was even more shallow than before.

"Look, I'm the fastest," Karl said. "I'll try to find a phone. Just in case."

"And I'm going to check over the car. Maybe even if I can't make it run," Gen said, "I could rig something with the radio."

"Do anything," Alice said. "We need help, fast."

Time seemed to freeze. Nathan wasn't aware of how tired he was. He slumped down and sat with his back against the heavy adobe wall. He didn't remember dozing off, wasn't really sure that he had. All he knew was that the next thing he remembered was the sound of a siren and the sky turning a paler shade of indigo.

Chapter Fifteen

Winter wasn't reasonable in Houston, Nathan thought. The day before, on the last day of school before the Christmas holiday, there had been snow. The city had hauled out snowmakers and had covered the lawn of City Hall with man-made snow. It had melted by late afternoon.

He had gone with his team, and a few other teams as well, and they had joked and played in the snow along with the rest of Houston's teenage population, but Nathan hadn't felt a true part of it all. He couldn't help remembering that night on the survival trek and their talk with Dr. Thompson afterward.

What he wanted to know was why Suki and two members of her team had gone off in a car and left the rest. Dr. Thompson had explained carefully that according to Suki, they had been trying to ferry their entire team in two shifts from the drop point to just outside the base. So they could win.

Nathan thought about that for a long time, and it didn't make any sense to him. Why shuttle the team if they had a car? Why not scrunch everyone in together? It might not be comfortable, but it was certainly faster. He mentioned it to the others a few days later, when no matter how hard he thought about it he couldn't explain the facts.

The team was sitting around the fountain, enjoying the warm weather and their freedom. Tomorrow they'd go home for the holidays, and when they returned they would elect a team captain and find out if they were going. It had been the only thing on their minds all day, and Nathan thought that asking about Suki's behavior was a way to think about something different. He couldn't take the tension anymore, and if he didn't change the subject, he was going to crack up.

It was Karl who spoke up. After all, Nathan thought, Karl did know Suki better than anyone else in their group did. He might even have some insight into her behavior.

"Suki is extremely competitive," Karl said.

"Tell me something I don't know," Alice muttered.

Karl waited for Alice to finish, and then went on. "Yes. But she isn't like anyone else I've met here. That girl is willing to do anything to get what she wants." Here Karl blushed a little. "I think she even acted like she liked me, like she wished I were on her team, so she could find out about what we were doing and how well. That's how Leon found out about Gen's vehicle and drained the battery. He admitted it in the hospital. The rest, I guess, was that the three of them were scouting the fastest route home. Then they'd ditch the car and pretend that they'd made it the whole way. Knowing Suki, that makes sense. The car was stolen, it turned out."

Lanie smirked. "Looks like I'm not the only one around here who knows how to use a slim-jim and hot-wire a car."

Karl looked at the floor. "I'm sorry," he apologized.

Lanie smiled and tapped him on the shoulder. "You know, Karl, for a preppie geek you're not too bad."

Karl smiled in return. "For a juvenile delinquent you're not too bad yourself."

"But stealing a car is crazy. And it's cheating," Noemi said.

"I guess she just didn't believe that," Karl said. "I thought it wasn't fair too. And I didn't believe it for a while."

"I guess so," Nathan said, although he wondered why someone like Suki just automatically pretended that a rule didn't exist if she didn't like it. Did she feel that way about atmosphere, say, or air pressure?

"And what about what her team did to me?" Gen asked. "That buggy would have worked beautifully. They deserve to get tossed out of the program!"

A scientist in a white coat with a NASA ID badge around his neck darted out between the buildings, noticed the fountain, and gave the group a suspicious look. He disappeared immediately into the next door.

"Here comes Thompson. Now we're in for it,"

153

Lanie groaned. Then she began to walk away. She almost made it out of the quadrangle when Dr. Thompson stopped her dead in her tracks, coming the other way.

"Hey, we didn't do anything," Nathan protested as Dr. Thompson arrived, Lanie in tow.

"Well, you did do something, but this time it happened to be right," Dr. Thompson said. "You rescued Suki and Vikram and Leon even after they had sabotaged your invention."

"Does that mean that Suki's out of the program?" Karl asked in a quiet voice.

Dr. Thompson shook his head. "I wish it did," he said curtly. "Unfortunately there are political concerns as well. They shouldn't be in a program like this, but that's life. If we don't play the politician's games, we don't get the money to go. And without money and support we're nowhere. You understand that?"

"No," Alice said firmly. "I do not understand. Someone like that, in an alien environment, she could get us all killed. She nearly got her own teammates killed, didn't she? One rotten egg can ruin the whole future of the colony."

"Grow up, Alice," Lanie said, shaking her head. "It's okay to lie and cheat and ruin someone else's work if you've got the bucks."

Science has always sacrificed to politics, Nathan thought. Galileo was tried and convicted by the Inquisition for insisting that the Earth revolved around the sun. Even Einstein had seen some of his finest work used to create the most terrible weapon

154

ever made. Compared to that, accepting Suki Long was a small price to pay for the entire Mars program. It was a price he could accept.

"So you know who's going?" Sergei asked, interrupting Nathan's train of thought.

"Of course," Dr. Thompson said. "We agreed, the three of us who have been working so closely with you kids, that it was cruel and unfair to send you off on vacation without knowing. So I came here to tell you."

"And?" Lanie asked.

"This group has always been the most trouble," Dr. Thompson said. "You break rules, you don't have any discipline, and you don't even apologize for it. On the other hand, you've got the two top math scores in the entire selection group, the third best overall performance in academics, and good practical skills. You also pulled off that rescue on the survival trek, which impressed the brass no end."

Karl blinked rapidly. "But what about the ratings that came out that said we were near the bottom?"

"Wait a second," Nathan said slowly. "I think I understand what this is all about. On that first day in the theater, you said we were all qualified, right? And I'll bet that's true. But you didn't want just smarts. All of us have that. You also wanted people who could pull together, who could put the group ahead of themselves."

"Something like that," Dr. Thompson said. "You kids are all used to working for grades and scores. But there aren't going to be any grades on Mars.

We wanted to see how you did without a rating system, so we turned the whole system upside down. The best teams got the worst scores. We wanted to see if you'd give up, if you were quitters. We wanted to see if you'd try your hardest no matter how hopeless it looked. That's the only kind of people we want to send to an alien environment."

"So now you can all go home and enjoy a few days with your families. And when you come back you'll have to elect a team leader and report before you're sent to the Kennedy Space Center at Cape Canaveral."

Dr. Thompson left them in front of the fountain while a busload of tourists filed past and dutifully took pictures.

"So what do you say?" Alice insisted, poking him in the ribs.

"Huh?" Nathan blinked. He didn't know what the conversation was about.

"What do you say to being team leader? We all agreed it made perfectly good sense."

"After all," Sergei said, "we're all good at what we do. But you're good at getting us to work together."

Karl looked up from the ground, smiled at Lanie, and then threw a hand over Nathan's shoulder. "Absolutely," he said. "Absolutely."

January

Mars. It was real, finally time to go, Nathan thought as he stood silently in the little waiting room. His teammates, all of them dressed in the red Mars program jump suits, were there, surrounded by their parents. And no one was saying anything at all.

Maybe it was that the good-byes had already been said, the last presents given. Noemi wore an unbelievable diamond necklace and earrings. Probably the very first person to go into space wearing a fortune from Tiffany's, Nathan thought. For once the crack didn't strike him as funny.

His mother stood next to him, trying very hard not to cry, as she had tried all during the vacation. Nathan felt bad for her, but he couldn't help thinking about what lay ahead. He was only part of the greatest adventure humans had ever undertaken, and he thought his mom understood that. She had even encouraged him. But there wasn't anything more to say. He was relieved as the coordinator told them it was time for them to get strapped into the shuttle that would take them up to where the three crafts for the journey had been assembled in orbit.

The *Nina,* the *Pinta,* and the *Santa Maria.* For sentimental reasons the US and Spain, along with all of South America, had proposed those names. It was one resolution the UN had passed by acclamation.

"This is going to make life awfully easy for history students in the future," Gen had whispered under his breath when the names of the ships were announced.

Nathan had thought the remark funny then. Now all that was important lay before them. The history of Mars was just beginning.

From the observation room, the parents, supervisors, teachers, and others who had been involved in the year-long search for candidates watched the silent shuttle board. Except for the parents, they had watched this same scene six times already and were scheduled for a good number more. No matter how many times, though, it was still something special to see the best and brightest of Earth leaving the home planet.

The giant boosters of the shuttle ignited, and even half a mile away the shudder and roar were perceptible. And then they were off, a small white speck cutting a perfect arc through the bright blue sky.

"Go, baby, go," someone said as the rocket sped out of sight.

Will Nathan, Alice, Sergei, Noemi, Gen, Lanie, and Karl really make it into space? Find out in their next exciting adventure, THE YOUNG ASTRONAUTS #2: READY FOR BLASTOFF!

For more information about The Young Astronaut Council, or to start a Young Astronaut Chapter in your school, write to:

THE YOUNG ASTRONAUT COUNCIL
1211 Connecticut Avenue, N.W.
Suite 800
Washington, D.C. 20036

Follow the odyssey . . .

THE YOUNG ASTRONAUTS

Follow Nathan, Sergei, Noemi, Alice, Gen, Lanie and Karl as they embark on their future adventures—a new one every other month!

September 1990:
THE YOUNG ASTRONAUTS #2:
READY FOR BLASTOFF!

November 1990:
THE YOUNG ASTRONAUTS #3:
SPACE BLAZERS

January 1991:
THE YOUNG ASTRONAUTS #4:
DESTINATION MARS

March 1991:
THE YOUNG ASTRONAUTS #5:
SPACE PIONEERS

Look for them at your local bookstore.